To Darry

The Lock of
Tianaju's Hair

Best Wishes

Pat Madden

24/11/2015

Pat Madden

© 2014 Virtualbookworm.com Publishing

"The Lock of Tianaju's Hair," by Pat Madden. ISBN 978-1-62137-558-6 (softcover); 978-1-62137-559-3 (ebook).

Published 2014 by Virtualbookworm.com Publishing Inc., P.O. Box 9949, College Station, TX 77842, US. ©2014, Pat Madden. All rights reserved. No part of this publication may be reproduced, stored in a retrieval system, or transmitted in any form or by any means, electronic, mechanical, recording or otherwise, without the prior written permission of Pat Madden.

Manufactured in the United States of America.

To my lovely, patient wife, Lorraine.

Special thanks to Scott Gallear for the cover illustration.

About the Author

Patrick Madden is a Welshman born in a little Welsh mining town called Blaenavon. His mother was Welsh and his father, Irish. He grew up being lucky enough to have the best friends one could ever wish for. Rugby and darts were his main hobbies. He played rugby for Blaenavon Harlequins R.F.C. and Abertillery R.F.C. He played darts for a local Blaenavon team called the Backroom Boys, but rugby was his passion. He loved every Saturday morning. It was the only time that he ever fled out of bed. After he wed a local girl, his married life took them to Scotland and then to Ireland. Now he is retired. He has five children and loves them all dearly. The inspiration for his first story, "A Name with No Meaning," came from his youngest daughter, Julie. He had always intended to write a follow-up story. While he was on holiday in Wales, he was lucky enough to take a photograph that became his inspiration to begin writing it. He would like to dedicate this story to his lovely, patient wife Lorraine.

The Lock of Tianaju's Hair

The beautiful Emerald Queen of Children sat at my bedside and began to tell me her lovely life story. When she had finished she gave me such a beautiful smile and said, "Sleep now little one."

I looked into her lovely green eyes and pleaded, "Please, can you tell me it once more?"

The compassionate queen held my hands and replied, "I'm sorry Welusa but I have to go now. There are many more children to visit tonight."

I held onto her hands and whispered, "You are so lovely, can you please give me something to remember you by?"

Her radiant smile lit up her beautiful face as she answered, "Well, I have never done anything like this before."

Then, using her first two fingers like a scissors, she cut off a lock of her wavy blond hair and slipped it into my nightshirt pocket. It felt lovely and warm and as I looked down at my pocket, I saw that it was sparkling with all different colours.

She laughed and said, "It's full of magic, but don't worry it will stop sparkling when I leave."

She kissed me on the forehead, stood up, gently opened up her wings and gracefully flew out through the glass of the window saying, "Good bye Welusa."

I rushed out of bed and opened the window. She was now sitting on her magnificent, large white elk Nabalion who was standing on the lawn in our garden. As he scraped his front right foot in the grass the beautiful queen told him, "I am ready Nabalion."

He then soared into the moonlit sky and was gone. I closed the window and climbed back into bed. My pocket had stopped sparkling now so I took out the lock of hair and found that it was tied with a green ribbon. Written on the ribbon was "Tianaju" with two little green crystals dotting the "i" and the "j" of her name. I jumped back out of bed and searched my bedside drawers for something to put it in. I found a little leather pouch and placed her lovely lock of hair into it. I put it back into my pocket and jumped back into bed. The sweet fragrance of her perfume lingered for quite some time, so I led there, enjoying it until it sadly faded away. I then sighed, turned over with my hand on my pocket, and fell fast asleep.

The following morning I woke up wondering, "Was it just a dream? Did I really see her?"

Then I felt the little leather pouch in my pocket. I slowly opened it up and said, "Yes, it's there, oh yes it really happened, yes, yes, yes."

I got dressed and ran down stairs to tell my mother. She was excited and said, "That's lovely son she must have liked you a lot, especially since she gave you a lock of her hair." She then laughed and said, "I'll tell you what, if you promise to be a good boy I will give you a lock of my hair too."

"Oh Mam," I said disappointedly. "You don't believe me do you? Just for that I'm not showing you the lock of hair."

I went straight up stairs and hid the pouch in a secret place in my bedroom. It stayed there until I was fourteen years of age, but I would look at it every night. On my fourteenth birthday, I took it from my secret place, put it into my shirt pocket, buttoned it over and never went anywhere without it again.

Before I carry on with my story, my name is Welusa Layovoy. I live in a small coal mining town called Afon Llwyd where the only Ironworks in the country is situated. The name Afon Llwyd is Welsh; it means, black or grey river. The source of the river comes from the Milfraen Mountain, which is only a few miles from where I live. It then runs past Kay's Slope and Big Pit. These are two collieries that are in the vicinity of my town. The river then passes through a washery where it is used to wash the coal. Hence the name Afon Llwyd. The black river then carries on down the valley into the sea.

———

During those years of growing up, I told quite a lot of my friends about the lovely queen and her story. Some believed me—mostly girls, and one or two boys. So fortunately for me, I was surrounded by pretty girls asking me to tell the story over and over again. I always told the story willingly, but I never told them about the lock of her hair. I also told them that one day I was going to write a book about her life story. One thing that always puzzled me though, was, why didn't the queen visit anyone else from the town?

From the day I was fourteen I stopped telling the story. I was determined to study hard and become a writer. Unfortunately, I couldn't concentrate in any of my school classes, not even my homework. All I ever thought about was the beautiful Emerald Queen of Children, her perfume and her lovely green eyes.

I left school when I was fifteen and got a job on Peter Evan's small farm. The farm was up on a hill near where I lived, everyone called it "The Atlas." It was tough enough work, but I enjoyed it. I especially liked working with a large Shire horse called Gwydion, ploughing up and harrowing fields, readying them for planting. Peter's lovely and kind wife June sometimes took in laundry to help some of the town folk who were struggling. With the money I had left, after giving my parents my keep, I bought: lead, pens, ink, paper and books to read.

On my sixteenth birthday, I began to write her life story and called it, "A Name With No Meaning." Although I knew her story off by heart, I can tell you now, it was not so easy putting it on paper. With all the spelling, punctuation marks, sentences, paragraphs and chapters it took me every night for six months. If it wasn't for the help of my childhood friend Cindy, who is now studying to be a teacher, my book would never have made any sense at all.

Cindy is one of the nicest and most happy girls I know. Unfortunately her legs were never strong enough for her to be able to walk for any great distance. When she was thirteen, her grandfather bought her a new invention called a wheel chair. Before that she used crutches. We grew up great friends and spent a lot of time together. Cindy is just a nick name. Her real name is Ella. The name Cindy came about when we were twelve. We were sitting on a bench alongside the black river when she asked me to tie her shoe lace up. I looked at her shoe and found that the lace was broken. So I took off her shoe and replaced her lace with one of mine. After I put her shoe back on I said, "There we are Cinderella." So I have called her Cindy ever since. I remember that day well because as I walked home my shoe kept falling off. By the time I got to the door there was a large hole in my sock. Although my mother darned it nicely for me, the lump was so uncomfortable that I threw it away the first chance I got.

It took twelve months before my book was finally published. During that time, I wrote out three copies of the manuscript and sent them to as many publishing companies. It was only after a publisher from America, who by chance was visiting our town, heard about the story that it was published. He was setting up a publishing house in London and assured me that he would virtually publish any good book. The man thought that mine was a very nice fairy tale for children, promising me a penny for every five books I sold to be paid once a month. I told him that it was okay with me because all I wanted was for him to publish it.

During the months that went by, I often wondered did I really see the lovely queen, was it just a dream, did my mother put the lock of hair into my pocket? She always laughed knowing that I carried it around with me.

"Mm," I thought. "I was only eight at the time and used to dream a load of old rubbish then."

So I became very despondent. All I ever thought about was the blond haired, beautiful fairy queen.

I lost interest in my job but still carried on doing a day's work. Then one day, a few months after my eighteenth birthday, I decided that I'd had enough of farming and would seek work in the city. So I told my boss Peter Evans what I had decided to do.

He tapped me on the back and said, "Yes I understand Welusa, you are just a young lad. It will be good for you to see a bit more of the country. There will always be a job here for you if things don't work out."

So late one evening in May I packed my bag and put on a good pair of boots, saying goodbye to my parents as I walked off into town. I was going to catch the eleven o'clock mail coach to Chepstow then make my way on to Bristol. I popped into the Market Tavern on the way to say cheerio to my pals. I had one or two glasses of lemonade with them and they all wished me luck in getting work. I left my pals around ten-thirty to catch the coach outside Tommy Walsh's blacksmith shop. It was sad leaving them, and I felt a bit miserable walking away as they waved goodbye. It was a lovely night and the shining moon brightly lit up the streets.

I walked down the town and across New William Street with my head down thinking to myself,

"I really hope it's not going to rain."

As I was crossing the old cobbled cross roads nicknamed "Coffin Corner," I saw a young lady standing opposite from me waiting to cross. She was wearing a white dress and a green hooded cape. As we walked towards each other she kept her head down as we passed. Then, a strange thought came into my mind, "I'd like to marry her one day."

Suddenly, after this strange thought, a warm feeling came over my heart. I clasped my chest and felt my shirt pocket tingling. I immediately spun around and there standing on the opposite side of the street was the beautiful queen.

She was smiling, holding out her loving arms to me. She had lowered her hood and I could see her lovely, long, blond, wavy hair.

I slowly walked over to her saying, "It's you, it's really you. I wasn't dreaming."

She replied, "Thank you for writing my life story. To show my appreciation, and as a reward, I am taking you to my home in Fairyland."

She touched my eyes and to my amazement I could actually see the moonbeams streaming down from the pure white full moon. She then lifted up her emerald wand from underneath her cape and waved it over my head. All I could see was a rainbow of colours all around me. As the rainbows disappeared, I saw the fabulous snow white elk Nabalion with the lovely smiling queen sitting on his back.

"Come on then, it's my birthday tomorrow. Are you coming or not?" she asked.

I felt as light as a feather now and replied,
"Bet your life I am."

Then with one stride and a jump I was sitting
behind her on the magnificent elk. The queen told
me not to worry for I would never fall off. She
leaned over, whispered something into Nabalion's
ear and we soared up into the warm air heading
towards the moon. As we flew nearer to it, I found
that the sparkling moonbeams looked as if they had
swirled into a cluster. The queen once again told me
not to worry as we were about to go through it. As
we passed through, it was like going through a soapy
coloured bubble. And then it burst. To my surprise,
the lovely shining moon brightened up as if it were
day, revealing a fascinating world below. At this
point, I knew I was in Fairyland. As we descended I
could clearly see a vast forest that stretched on for
miles and miles. Beyond this forest were lakes, little
cottages and what looked to be several cities and
towns.

We gently landed beside a small lake on a
hillside full of beautiful purple heather. As we slid
off Nabalion the queen said, "Welcome to
Fairyland. This hill is called the Blorenge and the
lake is Vanbolena Lake. The cottage over there is
Bryan the caretaker's cottage. Bryan and his wife
Annette look after all the animals in the winter and
save all the little trees in the spring. He also has a
small bird castle in his garden."

Tianaju held my hand and we walked across the
beautiful hill. As we walked, we eventually reached a
point where I could see that within the lovely valley
below sat a glorious looking city and I was amazed.

She squeezed my hand a little and said, "This beautiful city is Vanbolena, my home. Come on lets walk down the hillside—my mother and father are waiting to see you."

As we walked down a path through the heather, the queen informed me saying, "I would like it very much if you were to call me by my name, Tianaju, rather than by my royal titles."

I said, "Thank you Tianaju. You make me feel very honoured."

Vanbolena looked lovelier and lovelier the closer we got to it. The city was surrounded by a wall of beautifully coloured marble stones. At the entrance to the city was a large archway comprised of what looked like pearls. The two gates were made up of silver fairy figurines and were already open. As we walked through the splendid gates, there was a loud cheer as thousands of small fairies appeared out of nowhere. They had been hiding, waiting to surprise me.

They all cheered, "Welcome to Vanbolena, the home of Tianaju the Emerald Queen of Children."

As Nabalion came along side us, Tianaju said, "Climb up. We are off to meet my father and mother, who are the King and Queen of Fairyland."

We trotted off through the city streets that were bursting with the most lovely cottages, houses and churches I have ever seen. We traveled on until we reached a long, winding, steep road that would take us up to the tall Vanbolena Castle. When we reached the castle I was entranced by its magnificence.

There is only one way to adequately picture Vanbolena Castle: close your eyes. Think of all the loveliest castles you have ever seen or imagined in your life. Vanbolena Castle is far more beautiful.

The gates of the castle were open ready, and inside, lining from the gates to the main entrance, were two rows of Royal Guards saluting with their wands. As we approached the castle, two great big wooden doors were opened by a smiling, kind-faced fairy butler. He asked us to go ahead and enter, as the king and queen were eager to meet us. I was feeling very nervous now and Tianaju could see this.

She comforted me by holding my hand, saying, "It's alright. Don't worry. I will be with you all the time. I will never leave you."

This made me feel a lot better as we walked through the hallway together. The butler opened a door in front of us and announced our arrival to the delighted king and queen. They were standing on each side of a lovely fireplace in which a crackling log fire was merrily burning.

She introduced me to her father, King Drahol and her mother, Queen Roaniler. They both welcomed me into their home and to Fairyland. The king told me how much he loved the book and that I was to be his honoured guest.

Tianaju then introduced me to her twin sister, Princess Anoralee, her husband, Prince Salown, her brother, Prince Aiden, who is the captain of the Guards, and her two cousins, Princess Ellie and Princess Lilian.

After the introductions we all sat down and chatted for a while. It was fascinating to listen to them telling me all about life in Fairyland and that every fairy loved my book. I was so overwhelmed that I just sat there listening in a daze. Later, I was shown to my room by Laura, who was one of Tianaju's personal maids. Then, just as I was coming out of one daze, I was thrown back into another. I had never seen such a beautiful bedroom. My mother would have absolutely loved it. I flopped onto the nice soft bed and led there with my eyes shut thinking about the lovely sleep I was going to have that night.

I was only led on that lovely bed for about five minutes before there was a knock on the door.

It was Tianaju. "Come Welusa I will take you to the top of the castle. There is such a lovely view from up there."

She was right, the view was magnificent. The full moon had now dimmed back to normal and was shining down on the twinkling city below. It seemed as if it was gently caressing the roof tops with its sparkling silvery beams.

She looked at the moon, then turned to me and asked, "Isn't it lovely?"

I replied, "Yes it is, but it isn't half as beautiful as you and your lovely green eyes."

"Thank you," she said shyly.

Then, to my surprise, she told me that her eyes were blue up until the time she was christened then they turned green.

We were only up there for about half an hour before she excitedly said, "Come on it's nearly midnight. Let's go and enjoy the party. My sister will be waiting for me because it's her birthday too."

She held my hand and we went down to join everyone in the great hall. Before the party began she introduced me to four of her other cousins.

The first one she introduced me to was, Princess Stacey the Lost Diamond Fairy. She collects all of the lost diamonds from throughout the world and changes them into twinkles. Then, at night when young children are fast asleep, she gently drops one of these twinkles into each of their eyes. These twinkles last forever but no one can see them until the children turn sixteen. When they reach that age and fall in love, their eyes will only sparkle when they encounter true love. She then went on to tell me that a few years ago, while Stacey was collecting lost diamonds, she saw a small child throw a teddy bear away. She picked it up and brought it home. The teddy had a pocket in front of him and to her surprise there was a chestnut sprouting inside it. She planted the chestnut in Ginger's wood and with a touch of magic it grew into a castle. She now lives there in Chestnut Castle with her dear husband, Prince Roger. Princess Stacey now takes the little teddy with her everywhere she goes, and at night she uses his pocket to collect all of her diamonds.

Her second cousin was Princess Kirsty the Lost Book Fairy. She collects all the old books that people throw away and brings them back to Fairyland. She then cleans and sprinkles them with a little magic, making them lovely and new again. Then, the caring fairy delivers them to Santa Clause, ready for Christmas Eve.

The third and fourth very pretty cousins were blonde-haired, blue-eyed Princesses—Charlotte the Humming Fairy and Bobbi Mae the Fairy Tale Fairy. These exceptional Princesses are two of the very few fairies that don't need moonbeams in order to fly on. Princess Charlotte every night where ever there is a sad lonely child that cannot rest, she gently strokes their head and hums them a lovely fairy tune until they fall asleep. She then blows them a kiss that turns into a little daisy chain floating down onto their bedside table.

Princess Bobbi Mae also flies every night, visiting all the lonely grandfathers throughout the world. She comforts them by telling them her lovely stories. I was surprised to learn that she was very fond of one particular lonely grandfather from my home town. She calls him Grandad PJ Lawson. He looks forward to her visits once a week. He loves her stories so much that before she flies away, she blows him a kiss. This kiss instantly turns into a magic tiny star, which he catches and carefully puts into his pyjama pocket. The following week when she returns, the star changes into an invisible story book that only she can read.

Next to be introduced to me was one more very happy, bubbly fairy. Her name was Julia the Vanbolena Halloween Fairy. Every Halloween she flies around and does her best to make sure that the children are not too afraid.

At the party we had nice, tasty things to eat and later danced and played house games. It was great fun. Princess Ellie and Princess Lilian were exceptional dancers. They also won most of the house games too.

After the lovely party was over, I went to bed that night a very happy young man.

My visit to Fairyland caused great excitement amongst the fairies. For another week they held lavish balls and parties in my honour, making me feel like a king. Princess Ellie and Princess Lilian did their best to make my time in fairyland enjoyable. They insisted that I accompany them as they made their way to the top of the great tall castle, which is the nearest point to the moon. Once at the top, it was their job to send up into the Vanbolena sky all the teeth that Simone the Tooth Fairy had collected. They placed each tooth in the palm of their hands and blew them into the night sky, where they turned into twinkling stars. They then placed one in the palm of my hand and told me to blow. I felt a little embarrassed as I pointed my hand towards the sky. I was expecting the tooth to fall off as I blew, but to my surprise it traveled with speed into the night sky and turned into yet another twinkling star. The princesses explained to me that since the beginning of time, most of the stars in the sky belong to every child that left a tooth under their pillow. I was absolutely amazed to think that quite a few of those stars were mine. Thanks to the princesses, there was never a dull moment.

On one of the days, Tianaju, along with Nabalion, took me to the Enchanted Forest. She showed me her faithful friend Bellows' grave and tapped it three times before we left. She also took me to the amazing willow gates. When we arrived there, they were waving their branches as if they were excited to see us. They were massive and so dense that it was impossible to see through them. In fact, the whole forest border was this way. Tianaju told me that the forest border was invisible to the humans on the other side. I was really puzzled when she told me that, so I asked, "How can that be?"

She replied, "With magic."

I really enjoyed that day touring around most of the places from her story. It was fascinating.

The sun was beginning to set as we returned to the castle. We were so hungry that we went straight to the kitchen and helped ourselves to a sandwich. As we were sitting there, Laura came in to tell Tianaju that her parents wished to see her.

She walked away saying, "You stay here and finish your sandwich, I'll try not to be too long."

I asked Laura, "Will you stay with me and chat awhile until the queen returns?"

She replied, "Yes of course I will, Welusa."

We sat there chatting away for about half an hour until the kitchen door opened. I turned around and saw Tianaju standing in the doorway. She looked very upset as she said, "I am sorry Welusa but I am so tired, I just need to go to bed. Good night, I will see you at breakfast."

As she walked away I looked at Laura and she just shrugged her shoulders and said, "I know nothing."

I went to bed that night wondering what it was that upset her. I said to myself, "I hope it wasn't me they were talking about." You would never believe the things that ran through my mind. Eventually I fell asleep, until Laura woke me up with a knock on my door informing me that breakfast was ready.

I joined everyone for breakfast. Tianaju was already there, but seemed very quiet. As we left the dining room, Tianaju told me that she would be unable to spend the day with me as she had some unexpected royal duties to attend to.

So I spent the day wandering around the castle and grounds. It was enjoyable but I was still wondering what was troubling the lovely queen.

That night as Laura was packing my bag for my return home the next day, I asked her if she knew where Tianaju was. She told me that the last time she saw her she was heading up the stairway to the top of the castle. When Laura left, it was such a lovely night that I decided to go and look for the beautiful queen. I made my way up the stone spiral stairway to the top of the castle. When I arrived there I found her sitting on a bench wearing a lovely glistening yellow dress, but sadly she was in tears. I walked over to her and said, "Tianaju whatever is the matter?"

She looked up at me and her beautiful face looked as if she had been crying for some time.

"Oh it's nothing for you to worry about Welusa. I will be alright in a minute," she said wiping her tearful face with her wet handkerchief.

I told her, "Well it certainly doesn't look that way, so please tell me, why are you crying, because we are not going down until you do."

"Oh I am sorry Welusa that you found me this way."

I sat down beside her and gave her my clean dry handkerchief and insisted that she told me what it was that was troubling her. She wiped her face and began to tell me.

"Oh Welusa, this is so hard for me. You must believe me when I tell you it was not my original intention. I can still picture you all those years ago when you asked for something to remember me by, and I gave you a lock of my hair. Throughout the years, I always kept an eye on you, so when I found out about a year ago that you had written and were going to publish my life story, I was overjoyed. Your belief in me was heartwarming and I loved the thought of you writing my story. Thus with my father and mother's permission, I decided that I was going to reward you for your loyalty by bringing you here to my home in Fairyland for my birthday.

However, a few months ago something terrible happened that threw our land into turmoil. We needed help. Human help, to be exact. My father last night suggested that I should ask you for your help. He felt that your years of loyalty to me meant that you could be trusted. You can see now why I am crying. I feel so terrible about having to ask you to help us. I don't want you to think that was the only reason I brought you here. It was never my intention. I only wanted to reward you. However circumstances changed and I do feel in my heart, that you really are the only one we can ask. Please forgive me."

I held her hand in both of mine as I assured her, "Oh Tianaju, there is nothing to forgive you for. I am happy in fact I have never been so happy in my life. I understand how you feel and I believe that your intentions were genuine. So please don't be sad, just tell me what it is that I can do to help you. I will consider it an honour, and will even let you keep my best handkerchief."

She smiled, bowed her head and said, "You are so sweet. This is why I didn't really want to involve you."

I placed my hand under her chin, raised her head and looked into her sad but lovely eyes and said,

"I know that, but I am here now and eager to help. So come on, don't be afraid just tell me, please?"

She gave a big sigh then said, "Alright Welusa I will tell you."

I let go of her hands and sat back facing her and she began, "As you know from my life story the moon is of great importance to fairies. You also know what happened to the moon after my birth and how it affected the early years of my life."

I replied "Yes I remember."

She reached out and took my hand saying, "Well something terrible is happening to it again and once more it is beyond our magic to prevent it."

She squeezed my hand a little and shuddered asking, "Do you remember Ohibronoeler?"

I replied, "Yes I do."

She continued, "Well, when he chose to live with the cruel humans in Cleremun my father took his wand away and told him, that unless he changed his ways he could never return to Fairyland. He just laughed at my father and told him he didn't care and that one day he would get his revenge.

So four full moons ago he hid in his friend's home knowing that his youngest child's first tooth had fallen out. Being a fairy himself he knew exactly when Simone the Vanbolena Tooth Fairy would arrive to collect it. He would be the only one that could see her, even though she could be invisible at the time.

As Simone lay down her wand to search under the pillow for the tooth, Ohibronoeler pounced. He snatched her magic wand and grabbed the startled Tooth Fairy, bundled her into a sack and carried her off to his dreadful home. He imprisoned her in the same miserable, squalid room that he had kept me in. He tortured poor Simone into telling him all that was happening in Fairyland."

"She must have been terrified?" I asked.

She replied, "Yes, and he also found out about the title and privileges bestowed upon me. This made him angry and extremely jealous. He roared at her saying, Queen is she? I'll give her Queen. With her miserable locks of hair together with your wand I'll end the flight of all you silly fairies. I will swallow up every single moonbeam throughout the entire world. Yes, it will be your very own queen's hair that's going to snuff out the light of the moon."

The queen went on to tell me, "When Ohibronoeler captured me I was unconscious and during that time he cut off two long ringlets of my hair just for spite. He also pulled quite a lot of my hair out as he dragged me from room to room. So together with Simone's wand, my hair, and the late night thick mist from the river, he conjured up a magic spell and transformed himself into an enchanted misty, hairy dragon. For two nights, he roamed the sky swallowing up as many moonbeams that he could. His plan was to swallow up all the moonbeams in the world to prevent us fairies from ever visiting the children at night again. He also went around collecting coal dust along with soot from all the smokey chimneys, and then spat them into the moon. He knows that if the moon was black it would never shine again. However on the third night, after he changed into the dragon and took off into the sky, the tooth fairy escaped. She escaped the same way as I did, with the help of a squirrel. Before she fled away she was able to find her wand which he kept in his riding boot. Now without her wand he is unable to change himself back again. We ourselves cannot change him back, simply because, he is the only one that knows his magic spell. So he is quite contented roaming the skies as a broken misty hairy dragon during the day, and a full misty hairy dragon at night. He now travels the world swallowing up all the magic moonbeams and slowly trying to black out the lovely moon."

I was finding this a little bit hard to believe, but I looked at her, shook my head then asked, "What are you going to do? How are you going to stop him?"

She answered, "There is nothing we fairies can do to stop him. We are forbidden to use our magic to harm anyone in your world not even the dragon. The only one that can help us is a human, because the dragon is in your world."

I interrupted her then, saying, "Yes and that's me, but please carry on, I am even more eager now."

She sighed stood up and walked over to the turrets and said, "Well if you really want to help I would be grateful if you could deliver a message informing the four great winds about the dragon and his plan."

She went on to explain, "The only way to stop the dragon is with the help of the four winds blowing towards each other trapping him in the middle. Then hopefully they can find a way how to stop him."

I was puzzled now, so I walked over to her and asked, "How am I going to get, or even ask them to do that?"

She replied, "The only thing I can give you is the ability to see and talk to the winds, to Ohibronoeler, the animals, birds and the trees. I have already given you the ability to see the magic moonbeams."

I thought awhile then questioned her, "Why don't you ask the winds yourself?"

She answered, "The winds believe in fairies but they cannot see us. They can only see humans."

I was once again puzzled, so I asked, "Okay, but where are they? How do I find these winds?"

She sighed again before replying, "You must go to the North Pole of Scotland, the South and East Pole of England and the West Pole of Wales because that is where their sons live. You can explain to them what Ohibronoeler is doing to the moon. Inform them that without the moonbeams the moon will have no gravity pull on the seas. The seas will be calm causing the winds to lose their power and sadly cease to exist.

Therefore there will be no snow for the children to make snowmen, no ice to go skating, and no rain for water. Once you have told them this, you must then ask them to pass on the message to their great fathers."

I was surprised to hear this so I exclaimed, "Moonbeams pulling the seas!"

She answered, "Yes, it's the magic moonbeams that are the moon's magnetic pull on Earth. Without them, the moon will just drift away into space for ever."

I looked at the moon and said, "That's terrible! The whole world could perish."

I thought for a moment then asked, "Why do I have to tell all the four winds? Surely if I just told one of them he would tell the others, wouldn't he?"

She answered, "The four winds hate one another. They are constantly battling to be the strongest, but the North Wind always wins. He has reigned supreme for many years. Their sons are not very fond of one another either. This is why you must tell all four. If you begin with Soaker the South Wind's son, then Toaster the West Wind's son followed by Nipper the East Wind's son, then by the time you get to Howler the North Wind's son, all four of the great wind's will be beginning to feel their power weakening."

"Why will they be weaker?" I asked.

She answered, "By that time Ohibronoeler would have swallowed up a tremendous amount of moonbeams, weakening the moons gravity pull. This would make them realise their need to band together, or die."

"Well, we had better get going then," I told her as I touched her arm.

She turned to me saying, "That's enough, for now it's chilly up here. Let's go down for a cup of warm milk and inform my parents of your decision. We'll talk more about it tomorrow."

I was feeling excited but a little worried when I went to bed that night. While I lay there, mulling over the day's events, my thoughts turned to the next book I was going to write when I sat up shouting, "Yes, Oh yes, brilliant!"

I remembered that my next book was originally going to be from the moment she gave me the lock of her hair, right up until I finished the book of her life's story. I was so excited now with the thought of also being able to tell you about some fantastic adventure, an adventure that you will probably find hard to believe.

I was happy after that and fell sound asleep until the sun shining through the window woke me up.

Later that evening after dinner, Tianaju and I sat in the library discussing the dragon.

During our discussion, I asked the lovely queen if she was coming with me.

She answered, "No, unfortunately I cannot come with you."

I didn't ask her why, I just shrugged my shoulders and said, "Well how am I supposed to get to these Sons then? Do I fly or do I walk?"

She laughed a little and said, "You can't fly without wings and it will take you too long to walk. Nabalion will take you as far as your home. Waiting there for you will be a dapple grey stallion harnessed to a small coach. This stallion is the only one in the world that has a black wavy mane. His name is Lianga. He lives in your world but he belongs to me. He will tell you what to do and will take you to all the four poles where each son of the winds live."

I asked her, "Could I have a book of writing paper, ink and some pens. I intend to keep a diary of my journey every night?

She replied, "Yes, of course you can."

I felt better now knowing that I had transport, but disappointed she wasn't coming with me.

The lovely queen then said, "If you can be ready by midnight Nabalion will be waiting in the courtyard for you."

As we walked back down to our rooms she kissed me on my cheek and said "Thank you, I will be forever grateful."

I went into my room and sat down on the bed, thinking to myself, "Mm this seems like something impossible to me. Where is everyone? Am I dreaming or is she sending me on a similar task to the one she was given? If she is, then why? I am already christened."

Because my bag was already packed, I walked over and sat on the window sill ready to go. It was midnight now and I could see Nabalion walking into the courtyard. I had a last look around my lovely bedroom and went outside to meet him. I was pleasantly surprised when I heard him speak to me for the first time.

"Are you ready sir?" he asked.

I felt a bit silly at first then replied, "Yes I am."

As I was still very light, I jumped up onto his back quite easily. He stood there for a while, so I said to myself, "Why isn't he moving?"

No sooner than I said this I felt my chest getting warm and my pocket started sparkling. I quickly turned and looked towards the castle doors and there standing in the porch, was the beautiful smiling queen. She was wearing a yellow dress with a purple cape over her shoulders.

"Wait for me," she shouted.

I shouted back, "What! I thought you weren't coming."

She came running towards me saying "I was only kidding."

I was stunned for a second then asked, "Are you really coming?"

She laughed then answered, "Bet your life I am."

She jumped up behind me and put her arms around my waist.

I turned my head a little and asked her, "I thought you said that you couldn't fall off?"

She gave me a little squeeze and replied, "Well I might."

I tapped her hands and she said, "Let's go, Nabalion."

The magnificent elk silently rose up into the night sky like a bird. The king and queen were standing on top of the castle waving and wishing me good luck. So too were thousands of cheering fairies.

I felt like a million dollars now especially with her arms around me. It didn't take us long to fly out of Fairyland and gallop down the lovely moonbeams back home to Afon Llwyd.

We landed on the road just outside of town. Stood there waiting for us was the magnificent dappled grey stallion. His mane was long, black and wavy, tumbling down around his neck. He was coupled up to a small royal blue coach. I had never seen a coach quite like it.

Tianaju told me the coach was hers and that Nabalion had brought it there a few hours ago. We said good bye to Nabalion and waved until he went out of sight.

"Good morning your majesty it's lovely to see you again," said Lianga.

"Good morning Lianga my friend, it's nice to see you too," replied the lovely queen.

He now turned to me and said, "Good morning Welusa."

I replied, "Good morning Lianga," and walked towards the coach. I looked inside and there was a bag and a blanket on each of the two bench seats.

Tianaju pointed out, "These leather bags are fully waterproof. That bag there is mine; it has my clothes in it. The other contains weather proof clothing and food for the both of us. Your writing paper, ink and pens are in there too."

I threw my pack inside and asked, "Well, when do we start?"

She stepped up into the coach saying, "I have to get changed first, so excuse me a minute while I do so."

She reappeared, dressed for the journey, wearing a long blue heavy dress and a warm black cape.

I said to her "You look just like one of the ladies from the village now, but far more beautiful.

She told me that she would soon put a stop to that and bent down, rubbed her hands in the dust and patted her face. "How is that?" she asked.

I laughed and said, "Just a waste of time."

As we know from Tianaju's life story her wings are extremely supple and can easily fold down flat across her back underneath her cape.

I fetched my cape, put it over my shoulders and we both climbed up onto the driving seat, and away we went.

We traveled for a mile out of the town and pulled in alongside a woodland we call Foxes and stayed there underneath a large beech tree to rest for the night. We unhitched Lianga and settled down inside the carriage on each of the bench seats. As we lay there the beautiful queen explained to me,

"I am traveling with you just to keep you company and to tell you where the sons of all the winds live. If you remember, I cannot use my magic to harm anyone, or any living thing, not even the dragon while I am here. The mission has to be accomplished by you and you alone. All I can do is help you the best way I can, but not with magic."

I said, "Thank you I'm glad you came." She smiled and wished me good night. I wished her the same and we slept until dawn.

We awoke at sunrise and lit a small fire. After we had some toast and packed everything away, Tianaju informed me saying, "Soaker, the Son of the South Wind, lives high up in the rocks on the Isle of Wight. He draws in all the big clouds that collect the sea water, and then blows them down to his father at the bottom of the world. The strong South Wind then blows them back as rain clouds. He distributes them all over different countries at certain times of the year. Some stormy and some calm. So come on, let's get Lianga hitched up and head across the border then south in search of Soaker."

Before I tell you the tale of our epic journey, I must point out to you that it took us months of traveling. During that time we stopped and camped at numerous places, but far too many to mention them all.

Off we went following the trail down passed old Enoch's smallholding and onto Cwmavon road following the Afon Llwyd River. We were heading east to Gloucester then south towards the southern coast. On the way we met numerous people. Some were travelers, others were town folk. I had quite a lot of money that I had saved, so we stopped in some of the towns to buy food and milk for us and oats for Lianga at the local markets. It took us well over a week of traveling before we came to a place called the Cheddar Caves. This was an ideal place to stay for a day to freshen up and stay overnight. It was a lovely day so we stopped by the caves, unhitched Lianga and lay down on the grass for a while. Later we went to explore the caves. As we entered them Tianaju was greeted by hundreds of bats, "Welcome your highness Emerald Queen of Children. Welcome to our home."

She smiled and waved saying, "Thank you all, it's lovely to be here."

I must say I found it very strange being able to listen and talk to them, but got used to it after a while. The queen told them about our mission and that if Ohibronoeler finds out about it, he would try to stop us. When they heard about the dragon they all shuddered with fear. They knew what Ohibronoeler was capable of and how cruel he is to animals.

"We will keep a look out for him, your highness, and send messengers to warn you," said the caring bats.

We were about to leave when we heard someone further along in the caves counting. The bats told us that it was only the Log Saver, an old hermit who has relations in Shepton Mallet. He collects all the lovely logs he can find for his fire, but loves them so much he can't bring himself to burn them. Instead, he shivers away in front of a few burning twigs. He is constantly on guard from the fear of a legion of desperate log burners. So day and night he can be heard counting his large hoard of lovely logs. As we left the caves saying good bye and thank you to the bats, the hermit could still be heard counting in the distance. Then to assure us, Michelle an old bat, who must have been their leader's, wife shouted back, "Sleep well tonight, don't worry, we will watch over you."

When night came, and as we were sitting around a nice fire talking, Tianaju clasped my arm and whispered, "Look there he is. It's him, Ohibronoeler."

I looked up into the sky and sure enough, there it was. I could see it quite clearly in the moonlight. It was a broken pure white, misty, hairy looking dragon.

The frightened queen stood up and gasped, "He is swallowing up the moonbeams. Quick! Grab some blankets. We must hide in the caves before he sees us."

So we hurried into the nearest cave and sat down at the entrance to get our breath back. I suddenly thought and asked her, "What about the carriage and Lianga?"

She answered, "It's alright, Lianga is in the woods and the carriage is up there."

"Up where?" I asked.

She pointed and then I saw it. By magic she had put it up in the middle of an oak tree.

"Well no one can pinch it from up there," I said.

She laughed then assured me, "We are safe now. Come on, let's go in and lie down, the bats will warn us if there is any danger."

There were lots of dry leaves in these caves so I gathered them up and we lay down on them covering ourselves with the blankets.

As I lay there I mentioned to her, "Its awful dark in here. I can't see a thing."

She tapped me on my arm and said, "That reminds me of a promise I made about a year ago when I visited a young nine year old girl. When I arrived I found that she was singing herself to sleep. So I sprinkled some magic so that she wouldn't be afraid while I sat on her bed. To my surprise she didn't move, she just carried on singing. I spoke to her saying hello. She turned towards me and asked, "Who is there?" I then realised that she was blind. I told her who I was and that I came to tell her a story about my life. She was very excited, so I held her hand and told her my story. After I had finished she asked me, just like you did, to tell her the story once again. I explained to her that I had to visit other children that night. I went on to tell her that I had visited a young boy about her age some time ago. He is seventeen now and has written and almost published a book about my life. So I promised her when the book is published, I would come back one night with this book, so that her mother would be able to read my important life story to her every single night."

"That was a nice promise," I remarked. "You will have to give her a book then."

She replied, "Yes we will."

I turned over still thinking about the little girl and eventually fell asleep.

In the morning I was awakened by Lianga whinnying outside. I got up and found that the lovely queen had gone. I looked out of the cave and there she was, sitting around a small fire.

She waved and shouted, "Good morning Welusa. Come on down before your toast gets cold."

I gathered up the blankets and joined her for breakfast. Lianga was already hitched up to the coach, which by magic was back on the ground, and ready to go.

After breakfast we set off once more heading south for New Salisbury, a town that runs besides a river. After we traveled at least seven or eight miles there was a rain storm, so I told the queen to go inside out of the rain. I put on my cape and carried on down the trail which was now getting wetter and wetter. The rain lasted for most of the day, and it was late afternoon before the clouds broke, and the rain stopped. The sun now, was out once again and was drying everything up, including me. I carried on for about a mile until I saw an opening in some trees and thought it would be an ideal place to camp for the night. We set up camp, and enjoyed a nice cup of hot soup. Lianga had his oats then browsed around the trees. After a while a cuckoo, came flying through the trees and landed out of breath on a branch beside us.

She was looking very anxious as she struggled to tell us, "The dragon spotted after the rain storm and is looking very mean indeed. He is circling above you this very moment. What are you going to do your Majesty?"

She answered, "He can't harm us, but he will be wondering what we are doing. So we will have to be careful. Thank you for warning us Anne. Come Welusa! We must stay in the coach tonight until dawn. He will be busy swallowing up the moonbeams until then."

Before Anne flew away she promised to watch over us.

I was very tired now so we snuggled down in the coach and slept all night long.

At sunrise I woke up finding Tianaju was up again before me with the fire lit and making toast.

"Hurry Welusa we must make haste to New Salisbury. Isle of Wight is not too far after that."

Within half an hour we were on our way down the road again. Tianaju was inside the coach out of sight from the wandering dragon.

It took another few days before we arrived just outside New Salisbury. It was early evening so we camped under some trees beside a river. As we were sitting on the bank of the river, three men and a lady from the town came over to me and asked, "Where have you come from?"

I replied, "My friend and I have come from South Wales. We are going to the Isle of Wight to see someone."

The men looked all around, then one of them asked me, "Where is your friend?"

When I turned to Tianaju I found she wasn't there, but heard her whisper, "Shh," in my ear. I then realised that she was invisible, so I quickly stood up and pointed to Lianga saying, "There he is. He's my lovely dappled grey stallion."

Another of the men asked, "Would you like to sell me this horse sir? I have never seen a horse quite like him in my life. He is magnificent."

I replied, "No, no, he is my pride and joy, and even if I did sell him, how would I get to where I am going to?"

He answered, "We will give you another one instead."

I laughed and said, "Ha, no, no, I would never sell him, ever."

The locals walked around Lianga and said, "Well good evening to you sir and good luck on your journey."

When they were gone the lovely queen appeared again.

"Why didn't you tell me you would be invisible?" I asked.

She laughed and replied, "I forgot."

I laughed back at her and said, "Yeah, I bet you did."

During the night while we were sleeping we were awakened by a piecing cry. I could hear Lianga calling, "Get up Welusa there is trouble."

I dressed quickly and jumped out of the coach. There was one man trying to catch Lianga and the other was rolling around on the ground in agony. I picked up a stick and ran at the men shouting, "Get away from here, and leave my horse alone!"

One of them ran away while the other slowly hobbled off mumbling, "Rotten horse."

Lianga told me that they had tried to steal him, so he kicked one of them in the bottom.

I laughed and said, "Good for you, well done."

We were up early in the morning and made our way through the town and across the bridge over the river. We were heading now for the coast land of Hurst. It took us another day before we arrived there safely on the beach looking up at the lovely Hurst Castle. In between us now and the Isle of Wight, was a wide channel of rough looking water.

"How am I supposed to get over there?" I asked the queen.

She answered "Lianga will take you across, he can swim faster and stronger than any other animal, but it will not be easy, so hold on tight."

So I hid the coach and all our belongings in a cave except for the bag that contained everything we needed for our camp

I was never a very good swimmer, so I was a little bit worried as we waited for the tide to go out. "Don't worry you'll be okay, I'll keep you company." said my lovely comforting Fairy Queen.

After the tide went out the channel was a lot calmer making me feel a lot braver.

"Are you ready?" Lianga asked.

I replied, "Yes I am."

Then sighed as I jumped up onto his back. He walked into the channel and I was amazed by how strong he could swim. He could swim almost as fast as a fish. He swam so fast that his back barely went below the water. This was great for me because all I had to do was hold on to his long black mane. The water was cold but I got used to it quickly as we sped through the small waves. Tianaju was now the size of a small bird flying above us, singing all the way. When we arrived onto the island I was soaking wet but didn't care. I was exhausted, but safe now and on dry land.

I thanked my fabulous stallion for carrying me safely over and led down to dry in the warm sun. I fell asleep as I led there and woke up with a nudge from the queen.

"Wake up, sleepy head, it's time to go. We are off now to Black Gangs Rocks, the home of Soaker the South Wind's son. Come on, Lianga is waiting for us."

I was almost dry now so I picked myself up, stretched, and said, "Okay, let's go."

With her cape back on, she jumped up onto Lianga and I jumped up with the bag behind her.

We were now traveling over marshy moors heading for the other side of the Island. After about an hour or two we knew we were very close to where Soaker lived because we could hear him swish swishing every now and then. We could also feel the spray of the sea on our faces the closer we got. It was not long before Lianga stopped in amongst an old ruin that must have been an old lookout fort.

"We are here. Come, let's get down and walk," said Tianaju.

We walked through the ruins and there, up in the middle of a huge mountain of rocks, was the son of the South Wind. The only way I can describe him is that he looked just like a huge grey and blue plume of wavy long feathers, with a serious looking face and eyes.

As I stood there in wonder of this awesome sight Tianaju shouted, "Quick let's get back into the ruins he is about to blow, cover up your ears."

We ran just in time as the mighty Soaker opened his mouth and drew in every cloud from off the sea. They were all now full of water, and as he drew them in he swelled up into an enormous size covering all but a small part of the mountain. We watched as he filled up his cheeks and with one mighty blast blew them back out again across the sea down to his father at the South Pole. As he did so, he ripped up small waves along the way and sent them down too.

We decided to wait until after his next blast before I called out to him. I did not have to wait more than two minutes, before he let loose another powerful blast, exactly the same as the last one.

As soon as he had settled down to catch his breath I nervously called out as loud as I could, "Soaker, Soaker over here, I'm over here!"

I stood there constantly waving my arms. At first, I thought he didn't hear me until I saw his bewildered eyes turn my way. He growled at me then asked, "Who are you? How do you know me? How can you see and talk to me?"

I shouted over, "My name is Welusa I am here with a serious message from the Emerald Queen of Children."

He growled at me again and asked "Did you say the Emerald Queen of Children?"

I replied, "Yes she is here right beside me."

"What does she want?" he roared.

My throat was soar now from shouting but I managed to call out, "Can I come up to talk with you? It is too difficult to tell you from here."

The next thing that happened took me completely by surprise. I found myself flying through the air, as he drew me in and placed me on a rock on the side of the mountain. I anxiously looked over to him as he looked at me and said in a deep voice, "Tell me."

I told him all about Ohibronoeler and his terrible plan.

He roared out, "What! Why is he doing this?"

I informed him, "His intentions are to swallow up all the moonbeams to stop every fairy from visiting the children in the world. If he is not stopped he will succeed in his quest. The moon then will have no gravity pull on the seas, causing them to shrink back away from the shores. Your power will cease to exist and so will you. There will be no rain or fresh winds ever again."

With that he almost deafened me as he roared back, "Where is he? I will destroy him. Tell me, where is this dragon hiding?"

He was extremely angry now. So I warned him, "The Emerald Queen of Children has told me you cannot destroy him alone. He roams as a broken misty hairy dragon full of magic moonbeams. He would dodge every breath you were to blow at him, leaving you exhausted. The only way to destroy him is with the help of your father and his brothers blowing together. Together is the only way you can trap him in the middle. This is why you must notify your father or else he too, along with all the other winds, will cease to exist."

He was deep in thought now, then, I heard him mutter, "Mmm, I wondered why I was feeling a little weak lately. I used to fill up this entire mountain with one breath."

With that, he drew me back in, and gently blew me back over alongside the ruins and said,

"Tell her Highness that I am on my way."

He spun around facing the mountain, and with one almighty blast against the rocks, catapulted himself through the air and across the sea. I could see him thrusting himself further and further out across the ocean, spraying the whole coast with sea water as he disappeared out of sight.

"Phew I'm glad that's over," I said, as I looked around for the queen.

I felt a gentle kiss on my cheek and whoosh there she was, smiling happily beside me.

"Thank you, my brave soldier. I am very pleased with you. Come, the weather's fine, so let us make camp here in the ruins for the night."

We set up camp, enjoyed a warming meal and discussed where we were heading next. We decided that we would go back up through England then head west through Wales to the Island of Anglesey. This is where Toaster the son of the West Wind lives.

We had a sound sleep that night and were up early the next morning trotting off back across the moors. We rested at the same place as where we arrived onto the Island. It was misty but I could still see Hurts Castle in the distance. The tide was already going out so I mounted Lianga and we slipped into the channel. When we were almost across we were instantly engulfed by a thick sea fog. I couldn't see a thing. I heard Tianaju telling me, "Don't worry Lianga is quite capable of seeing through fog."

I looked up and as I did so, I accidentally slipped off into the water. I was still holding onto Lianga's mane and trying to get back on when everything went black.

The next thing I knew, I was lying on the beach, coughing and spluttering, looking up at the beautiful queen. She told me with a lovely sympathetic voice. "You were hit by an old floating log and disappeared under the water. Lianga had to dive down and drag you to shore. So rest now for a while until you are fully recovered."

After an hour I felt myself again and walked over to the waiting queen who was sitting in the coach. "Are you okay now Welusa? Are you well enough to travel?"

I replied, "I am fine now, come on let's go to Wales."

We climbed up onto the driving seat and away we went at full pace. Lianga is as fast as any normal horse, but unlike them, he is able to keep up the same pace for hours. The only time he stops galloping is when we meet people on the side of the road and through the towns.

Tianaju did not mention Ohibronoeler again until one day after we stopped a few miles outside New Salisbury for a rest and refreshments.

As we rested she told me, "The fog on the sea was Ohibronoeler the misty hairy dragon. He must have seen us on the Island and was probably wondering why Soaker had raced away across the ocean. He knows we are up to something, and will do his best to find out what it is."

It was late now so we set up camp and slept until the morning.

The next day the weather was dull but it was fine, so we set off trotting through the quaint little town of New Salisbury. It looked as if there was a market in the town square that day. So we both thought it would be a good idea to buy some more supplies for our journey. We had a good browse around and purchased what we needed. As we were walking back to our coach a man grabbed Tianaju's handbag and ran off in front of us towards his accomplice. Immediately Lianga reared up startling the man making him drop the bag and run away. I quickly ran and retrieved it and handed it back to the thankful queen. We climbed up onto the coach and made our way out of town. As we trotted along I looked at Tianaju and said, "Those men were the same men that tried to steal Lianga the other night".

She asked, "How do you know?"

I answered, "I noticed that one of them was holding his bottom as he ran away."

She burst out laughing and so did I. In fact we laughed all the way out of New Salisbury and for a few miles more.

It took us two days to reach a small forest just before the Cheddar Caves. So we set up camp again and sat around a fire watching the flickering flames. It was dusk now and Tianaju was worrying about the dragon. The moon was not full any more so she knew he would be up to some sort of mischief. So nervously we bedded down in the coach that night hoping that he would stay away.

We awoke happy in the morning, surprised to know that we had slept, undisturbed, all night.

After breakfast our happy feeling soon disappeared. Anne the cuckoo arrived again with a message.

She told us that last night as a few young bats were playing outside, the dragon swooped down covering them with thick fog. Ohibronoeler demanded that they tell him exactly what we were doing on the Isle of Wight. They told him everything, because they couldn't see and were terrified that he would not go away. We thanked Anne for warning us and told her to tell the bats not to worry, as we understood how frightened they must have been.

I said to the queen, "I am not afraid of him, so come on, let's go."

We climbed up onto the coach and raced off up the road passing by the Cheddar Caves.

It was the following afternoon now, and by this time we had passed through Bristol and were camped up on the grass verge beside the River Severn. After studying the treacherous looking muddy river, we decided that we would not risk swimming over it because of its muddy banks. Instead we decided to go back to Wales through Gloucester, the same way we came. So we stayed there for the night to travel early the next day.

A wet miserable drizzly morning waited for us as we woke. Because the clouds were looking grey, we set off prepared for a storm. Fortunately for us, it turned out that the storm clouds blew away over to the west. However, as we were approaching Gloucester, we were suddenly swamped by a thick fog that slowed us down to a walk.

Tianaju held my arm and said, "It's the dragon. He's here."

Then there was a slow, deep, nasty sounding voice saying, "So you are back again Tianaju? You will never succeed with your lies and deception."

"Go away Ohibronoeler," she told him.

"Yes go away," I shouted too.

A more mellow voice now spoke to me saying, "Ah! You can hear me? I know you Welusa, you are a good fellow but you have been deceived by a cunning fairy. She is not even a queen. The story she told you happened to me not her. She was jealous of me, so she got her father to turn me into a dragon and banish me into your world. Help me Welusa? Give me her wand, so that I can go back and visit the children again."

Then, a slithering misty hairy arm, holding out its claw like hand, appeared beckoning before me.

"Don't listen to him. He is trying to trick you," warned the queen.

I reassured her saying, "It's Okay. I don't believe him."

I looked up and said out loud, "You once told Tianaju that it was the beginning of the end of Fairyland. Well it's my turn now, so I am saying it's the beginning of the end of you."

When I had finished, he roared back, "You fool, you will never beat me, and neither will the winds. I have a plan that no one knows about. So carry on wasting your time Welusa, because the pretty one is just using you. Once I have defeated the miserable winds she will leave you without even saying goodbye, ha, ha, ha."

He then drew his claw back into the fog and stayed there surrounding us all the way into Gloucester. We set up camp in some woods just outside the city and by that time the fog had lifted. Ohibronoeler must have decided to go elsewhere, but before he went, he managed to say, "Leave her Welusa before it's too late."

He then drifted up into the sky and headed westward to Wales. We lit a fire and sat down side by side sipping some juice discussing the taunting sneaky dragon.

While we were sat there I was thinking about New Salisbury when my old school pal came to mind. So I suggested, "In the morning we should head for Ragged Castle. My school pals Lord Rabry and Lady Meryl live there. They were childhood sweethearts and moved to the castle, from Salisbury estate Varteg, after they were married. They live there alone so I'm sure that he would be more than happy to let us camp there for a night."

She agreed, "That sounds a good idea. Do you think I could have a bath there?"

I replied, "Well I don't see why not, but what about your wings? If we go inside you will have to take your cape off."

She answered me slowly, "Let me worry about that."

I went on to explain, "My friends know your life story from my book. They also know your name. So to save you being asked a lot of questions I'll make up a different name."

I then went off looking for some logs to keep the fire alight. When I returned I found that Tianaju was very quiet and deep in thought.

I said to myself, "She must be thinking of how she can hide her wings. So I'll let her think awhile."

She was still very quiet as we settled down in the coach to sleep. I lay there for a while then asked, "Are you alright?"

She answered, "Yes I'm okay."

So I wished her good night and she wished me the same. Soon after I felt her hand tap me on my side. I turned, held her hand and asked, "What's the matter? I thought you told me you were okay."

She answered, "Do you remember when Ohibronoeler told you to leave me?"

I replied, "I remember. Why?"

She softly squeezed my hand and asked very sadly, "Well, will you leave me and the mission?"

I gave a little laugh, gently squeezed her hand back and said, "Well I might"

She gave me a poke in the side and said, "Oh you!"

We were up early in the morning and ventured out to find our way to Ragged Castle. I asked quite a number of people on the way for directions and they were all very helpful.

During the afternoon the dragon was back again, being tormenting and slowing us down.

"Welusa, where are you going? Oh yeah I know where you're going. Out, of your mind and back. You must be out of your mind to listen to the devious queen of heart breakers."

We took no notice of him and just let him rabble on talking nonsense. So unfortunately because of his constant torments, it was a miserable week of searching, before we eventually found the castle one evening before the sun went down. As soon as the sun went down the dragon left us and headed west for Wales.

It was only a small castle, probably the size of a fort, surrounded by trees. Eventually after searching, we found the gates and trotted through and up the drive way, stopping in front of the entrance door. I jumped down, and before I could knock on the door, it swung open. There beaming broadly, was my surprised looking school pal Lord Rabry. He greeted me with a hug and said, "It's great to see you." He then joked; I didn't think you would be speaking to us again now that you are an author."

I gave him a gentle punch on the shoulder, laughed and said, "Well I might, for a few shillings."

He laughed back and asked, "What brings you here? Is that your pretty wife up there on the coach? Put your horse in the stable around the back and bring her in and your bags. Go, go on hurry, I'll tell Meryl, she will be pleased to see you."

So we took Lianga and the coach around to the stable, unhitched, fed, and watered him, gave him a nice little pat and wished him good night.

We went back around to the castle door and into the arms of Lady Meryl my pal's lovely wife.

"Welcome Welusa, it's lovely to see you and this must be your beautiful wife?

I introduced her saying "Yes, err I mean, no, no she is not my wife, this is Evely Seloy, an old friend of mine."

Lady Meryl invited us to take off our capes and to go into the sitting room by the fire. I suddenly remembered about Tianaju's wings so I looked at her. She just smiled, took off her cape, and gave it to Lady Meryl to hang up. To my surprise there were no wings to be seen. So I handed her ladyship my cape and our bags and we went and sat down by a lovely fire.

Lady Meryl came in and told us, "I've taken your bags up to your rooms. Rabry shouldn't be too long he has just popped back outside to collect his tools. The shed he put up last week fell over this morning. Feel free to do as you wish while I go and make something nice for supper."

Before she went I asked her, "Would you mind if Evely took a bath to freshen up please Meryl?"

She answered, "Of course, silly me, I should have asked her. There is already a large pot of boiling water by the kitchen fire. If you give me a minute I will fetch her bag back down, light the fire in the bathroom and set up the bath tub in front of it."

When she went away I asked Tianaju, "Where, are your wings"

She replied, "Magic."

I sat back and said, "Ha, I should have known better."

She explained to me that her wings were no longer there, but if she needed them they would come back but invisible.

She then held my arm and asked, "Who did you say I was? Where did you get that name from?"

I sat back up, whispered in her ear, and said, "Magic."

She gently pushed me away, laughed and said, "Ah you!"

Lord Rabry came in with some logs and nearly dropped them when he caught sight of her sitting next to me.

"Wow! You certainly picked a beautiful wife? Where did you find her?" he asked jokingly.

I answered by introducing her, "This is Evely Seloy a very dear friend of mine. I am helping her find someone."

"Well I am very pleased to meet you Evely. Both of you must spend the night with us. Now sit yourselves back down."

We sat back down only to get up again as Lady Meryl come in simultaneously and told Tianaju that the bath was ready. So she went away to have her bath, while my old school friend and I chatted and laughed about days gone by.

He reminded me, "I never once beat you at cards."

I laughed and joked, "Yeah, you were always hopeless. You couldn't even shuffle tidy."

Her ladyship came in and told us supper was ready and that Evely wouldn't be too long. She was just drying her hair. So we joined Lady Meryl in the kitchen where the table was laid with bread, cheese and bowls of hot soup. As we sat there waiting I suddenly thought to myself, "I hope she is not going to come in wearing that yellow dress."

Then I gave a sigh of relief because when she did come in she was wearing the same clothes that we had arrived in. It didn't make much difference anyway, because with her looks and her now clean long blond hair, she looked fabulous. I could see that my old school pals were amazed when she entered the room and sat down beside me.

After a lovely supper we cleared the table and the four of us washed up. We then chatted by the fire side in the sitting room until bed time. Lady Meryl led us up the stone spiral staircase and showed us to our rooms at the top of the castle. We said good night to one another and retired to our beds for a much needed sleep.

I was awakened in the morning by a knock on my bedroom door. It was Tianaju saying, "Come on it's time to get up."

I replied as I jumped out of bed, "Okay I will be there in a minute."

I got dressed and we went down to the kitchen where breakfast was waiting for us. We ate heartily and then said our goodbyes. Lord Rabry and Lady Meryl came with us to the stables and helped us hitch up Lianga to the coach. We climbed up onto the driving seat and said, "Thank you and goodbye my friends."

They followed us out waving and shouting, "Don't forget to come back soon."

The night before, as we were chatting, I asked them which road was the quickest to the Isle of Anglesey. They told me to take the road to Welshpool first, and ask there. So that was where we were going to next.

We raced on until stopping after midday for a rest, a drink and a sandwich. I was tired now so I lay down on the grass to sleep. I was only asleep for five minutes before we were surrounded once again by the tormenting, thick, misty, hairy dragon.

Tianaju and I got into the coach, led down and told Lianga to walk on. There wasn't any need to guide him because he knew exactly where he was going.

All the afternoon, and up until the evening, Ohibronoeler taunted us with the same annoying nonsense. Then as dusk came, he slithered off, and headed towards the red sun set in the western sky. Tianaju was tired now, mostly because of the constant nagging dragon. So we decided that was enough traveling for the day, and set up camp for the night.

A lovely sunny day greeted us when we awoke, and it stayed that way for a few days. The dragon was nowhere to be seen which made our journey to Welshpool thoroughly enjoyable. We only stayed there to ask our way and to buy some milk. A kind elderly gentleman told us to take the Oswestry and Bangor road. After that, we only had to cross the Menai Bridge to the Island.

The roads were very hilly now, with lots of winding bends. We stopped several times to talk to local dwellers. Some were inquisitive, others were just happy to have a chat. One kind lady gave us a mug of fresh milk, some eggs and wished us well. The only one that did not wish us well was Ohibronoeler. He was back tormenting us every afternoon before we finally arrived somewhere near the bridge. As usual the menace left us and headed off towards the setting sun. We were happy that he was gone, so sleep came easily to us once again that night.

The following morning we set out at dawn and tracked over the long bridge and onto the breezy Isle of Anglesey. We traveled around the bumpy coast line until midafternoon then stopped for a rest above some white cliffs looking out towards the sea. It was lovely sitting there watching the birds and the waves rolling in and out. We sat there for about an hour until I saw something approaching from way out in the sea.

"It's him, it's Toaster. Wow! Look at him Tianaju."

"Yes I see him. He is so lovely," she replied as she held her hand over her eyes.

Once again, the only way I can describe him is, he's a huge mass of shimmering heat waves shaped like a ghost with a kind face. As we watched him rise into the air, he began to sweep back and forth the sky line. He was gently drawing in his breath the whole time, and getting larger and larger with every sweep. You could feel the warm air over us as he drew the sun's rays in towards him. Then, he turned around and with a mighty blow, blew the lovely heat waves westward across the sea to his father the West Wind. His father in a gentle breeze will blow them, along with his own, around different parts of the world.

I asked the queen, "Do you think he will hear me if I call out to him?"

She answered confidently, "Yes he will hear you quite clearly."

I waited for him to turn around ready to sweep again before I shouted, "Toaster, Toaster over here!"

The massive lovely wind stopped and looked towards me as I waved and called. He stared a while then rushed at me looking very serious. He stopped before he reached the cliffs and glared at me.

"Who are you? What do you want?" he asked in a deep, loud and hollow voice.

He wasn't looking so happy now and I was feeling very warm from the heat of his breath.

I took a deep breath before I replied,

"My name is Welusa. I have a message from Tianaju the Emerald Queen of Children."

He came closer now and raised his voice even louder and bellowed, "The Emerald Queen of Children. You tell me you have a message from the beautiful queen. Why should I believe you?"

I backed off a bit and answered, "Well I know that all you winds cannot see her, but she is beside me. So can I relay her very serious message please?"

He too backed away, and as he drew in his breath, I was lifted up, and placed on a tiny island out in the sea. He glared at me again and said, "What does she want? If I find that you are trying to trick me this is where you will stay."

I told him exactly the same as I told his cousin.

"How can I be sure you are telling me the truth?" he asked as he glared at me again.

I remembered what Soaker had said about losing some of his power.

So I asked him, "Have you been feeling weak lately?"

He pondered a while and answered, "Come to think of it, these last few weeks I have been getting tired. Also, I remember now, I have seen this dragon roaming around the sky. Mmm..."

After saying that, he whipped me up and placed me back beside the coach again.

He now said in a meaningful voice, "I will give my father her message. Now get behind those rocks."

He then drifted way back out from the shore, drew in his breath and blasted out a mass of flames that propelled him westward and out of sight over the Irish Sea.

"Phew! That was a long way out there on that island Tianaju. I thought he was going to leave me there."

Then, before I could say any more, she flung her arms around me giving me a hug, and said, "You are so brave and courageous. Anyone else would have been shivering in their boots."

So I didn't mention to her how scared I was. I just pretended that I wasn't.

"Well," I said to the hugging queen, "Let's make camp and recover before we plan our next route to the third son."

Tianaju knew that he lived somewhere off the coast of Scarborough. So we decided to head for Chester and ask there.

It was noon the next day before we set off along the coastline. It was beginning to cloud over so the sooner we got off that Island the better.

I sighed and said to Tianaju, "I suppose it won't be long before the menace will be upon us again."

She looked at the sky and agreed, saying, "Yes, we must make haste. Once he finds out that we have been successful in convincing Toaster, he will be extremely angry."

We had only traveled a few miles more when it started to pour down with rain. Then, like a blanket dropping from the sky Ohibronoeler was on us, even thicker than before. He had swallowed up a load of smoke that he had probably collected from a nearby town. It was almost impossible to see now, plus the smoke was making us cough and our eyes run. The stifling smoke was also making Tianaju quite sick. It was no use telling her to fly above the dragon because it was raining.

So, I suggested, "Fly over to the bridge Tianaju, shelter, and wait there for me until he has gone. Don't worry about me I will be okay."

She agreed saying, "Alright, but if you are in trouble, call me. Take my handkerchief and cover your mouth from the smoke."

Then with a sprinkle of magic, she was the size of my little finger and was gone.

"Blimey I wish I could do that," I said to myself out loud.

I put Lianga's food bag around his nose to help him filter the smoke.

He thanked me and said, "The smoke will not last for long, so keep your eyes closed. I will let you know when it's cleared."

So I did just that and I also covered my nose and mouth with Tianaju's handkerchief. I soon forgot about the stifling smoke, because the beautiful smell of her pretty handkerchief made me feel wonderful. All I could think of was her. We slowly trekked on for about another mile until the smoke had thinned out. Then, tragedy struck, we had hit a stone that dislodged the iron ring from around the rear left wheel. I stepped out from the coach, collected the iron ring and looked around.

I said to Lianga, "All I can do is to take off the wheel and temporarily replace it with those broken branches from that tree over there."

Lianga replied "That's a good idea. There are quite a few there so get them all just in case."

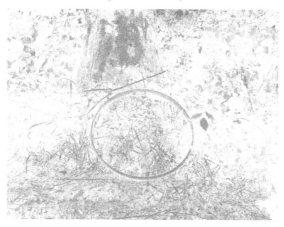

So I did, and with the help of Lianga, pushing his rear quarters against the side of the coach, I was able to take the wheel off quite easily. Then with the aid of my belt I tied it onto the front right hand corner of the coach. I then took a strong branch and tied it to the axle with Lianga's bridle reigns.

Next I collected some stones and placed them on the right hand side of the front bench seat. This helped to balance the coach as Lianga moved away. It worked a treat so I hitched him up and balanced it even more by sitting on the right hand side of the driving seat. I was soaking wet now but happy that we were up and running again.

"Phew," I said to myself. "That was hard work. Walk on Lianga," and off we went.

All of the time, that I was repairing the coach, I was constantly tormented by Ohibronoeler. His taunts were, "You'll never do it, you are fools, give up, the branch will break, and you are putting the stones on the wrong side. His bridle is rotten, phew I can smell it from here, get rid of it, burn it and the coach, it's full of fleas. Tianaju is dead; you are just wasting your time."

The branch held up fine and we made good head way. It was early evening when we arrived at the bridge and by then I had to change it for the third time. As I jumped down to replace it, I could feel my pocket tingling. I looked up and there she was, with that lovely smiling face of hers. I hugged her and said, "I'm so happy to see you again."

She replied "I am happy to see you too, Welusa."

With that, our tormenter shouted, "Ah! Rubbish, what a load of rubbish. What a pair of sloppy love doves. She doesn't mean it, she's just conning you that's all. Listen to me Welusa, I know her. I told you once before, that when I have defeated the miserable winds, she will leave you without even saying goodbye."

I shouted out, "Go away fool, I thought you said she was dead."

He was enraged and shouted, "WELL SHE IS TO ME! Besides she will die and so will you and your silly old horse."

After saying that, he gave a hideous laugh, took off into the sky and tore off out of sight.

"I am glad he's gone," said Tianaju.

"So am I," I said, as I began to replace the worn out branch.

We decided to go into Bangor to find a blacksmith. It was only a few miles away, but by the time we arrived there the blacksmith was closed along with all of the stores.

Tianaju asked, "Do you think we could get a room at the Inn for the night? I could do with another bath after all that smoke."

My reply was, "Yes, if that is what you want, come on let's find one. I need to dry my clothes too."

I found an Inn and with a sprinkle of magic Tianaju was invisible again. I went in and told the Inn keeper about my misfortune and booked a room for the night. I also asked him if I could have a bath and did he have stables for my horse.

He answered, "Yes, my wife will boil some water and prepare a bath in the washroom. The stables are around the back. My lad will attend to your horse and coach. In the morning he will take your wheel over to the blacksmith for repair."

I thanked him then his wife showed me to my room. The room was bare but had a nice little fire burning in the hearth. The bed was a bit lumpy but okay. So I sat down by the fire chatting to the invisible queen, while we waited for the bath to be ready. We didn't have to wait long before there was a knock on the door. It was the Inn Keeper's wife saying, "Your bath is ready sir."

I replied, "Thank you that's fine." I then looked out of the door and said to Tianaju, "Well, I suppose you know where the wash room is, so go on then, hurry, there is no one about. I will hide here until you've finished."

"Okay," she replied. "I won't be long."

While I waited for her to return I made up a few sandwiches for later on. I put them on the bedside table and sat down by the fire. I was sitting there far away thinking, when my pocket started sparkling again. I looked up and there she was, looking clean and shiny.

"I've finished, it's your turn now, the water is still hot," she informed me as she began drying her hair.

I had a think for a while, "Well, I suppose I could do with one." I pondered, "Umm, yes, okay, I will."

So off I went and was glad that I did, for it was lovely. After our bath we both felt clean and refreshed. We enjoyed our sandwiches and went to bed. I slept in the bed and Tianaju slept on the floor. No, no, I am only kidding. In fact, it was the other way around. Sleeping on the floor didn't bother me at all, because I was so tired I fell asleep straight away.

It was mid-morning before we awoke and had a quick snack for breakfast. I packed my bag and went down stairs. The Inn Keeper told me that my wheel had been repaired and was at the Blacksmith's. I thanked him for his kindness and paid him the bill.

When I arrived at the blacksmiths shop, Lianga was already hitched up to the coach. The wheel was repaired and now safely back on. I was so happy with the blacksmith, for doing such a very good job; I gave him an extra penny on top of his bill. I thanked him but before I left, I asked, "Could you tell me the best route to Scarborough please?"

He answered, "It's a long way across country lad. You must head for York which is about half way, but be careful. The Yorkshire moors are treacherous, especially in the fog."

I thanked him and he wished us, "Good luck and safe journey."

As soon, as we were clear of Bangor, Tianaju, was her normal self again sitting beside me.

"Ah there you are, I thought you had left me!" I joked.

She tapped my knee and looked up at the sky and predicted, "It's going to rain again so I will go inside to keep dry."

She was right, because no sooner than she was safely in the coach, it poured down. It didn't bother Lianga much, in fact, he loved the rain. It kept him cool as he galloped along, stopping only for a drink, and some grass.

We traveled on for six, miserable, wet days, but thankfully during that time the dragon for some unknown reason, was nowhere to be seen. So that made our journey to the Yorkshire moors a bit more bearable. As we climbed up the hill and onto the moors, I saw that they were exactly as the blacksmith described them to be. To make it even worse the moors were covered in fog. It was real fog this time and not Ohibronoeler.

I told Lianga, "Go steady take your time. We don't want another broken wheel again, especially up here. This place is so foggy and very creepy too."

He replied, "Yes this track is extremely wet and bumpy. It is the worst road I have ever been on in my life."

We rocked and rolled for at least a good hour, before we were swamped by the laughing dragon again.

He sniggered saying, "Dear, dear, dear! I'm back again, what a shame, ha, ha, ha you'll never make it this time Welusa. You will die in these bogs. Your fancy queen cannot save you, she is not allowed."

As he followed us, there was a terrible smell. He must have collected all the rotten smells around to stink us out.

I told Tianaju, "Fly above the fog until we get to the end of the moor's road. He will be gone by then seeking moonbeams."

She replied, "Alright, I hate horrible smells. Use my handkerchief again Welusa. Be careful. Remember to call me if you are in trouble."

Once again, with a sprinkle of magic from her wand, she was gone. It was almost unbearable now, as Lianga and I slowly tracked on, with the fog, the dragon and his stench.

As we made our way for about an hour I heard Lianga coughing.

I stopped and said, "Whoa! Lianga Whoa, I'll put your food bag around your nose. It will help filter the horrible smell."

As I climbed down from the driver's seat my foot got tangled in the reigns. This made me fall head first into a ditch full of water. Lianga cried out, "Are you alright Welusa?"

I answered him, "Yes, don't worry, I'm soaking wet, but okay."

I got his food bag from out of the coach and walked around and put it on him saying, "How is that? Does that feel better?"

He answered, "Yes, thank you, this is much appreciated."

Then, as I turned to go back to the coach, Ohibronoeler roared loudly. This startled me making me step back, lose my balance and fall into a slimy bog up to my waist. As I struggled to get out, I found that the more I did, the deeper I was sinking. I was helpless as the dragon whispered, "Poor old soul, what a way to die. I told you Welusa, it's the end. No one can help you now. Goodbye forever. I am very sorry for your trouble Welusa, I really am. I am ever so sad that I will never see you again, boo hoo hoo. Oh where's my hanky? Has anyone seen it?"

After saying that, he took off, leaving me slowly sinking further down. It was impossible for Lianga to turn around to help me so he cried out for Tianaju. She was with me in a flash and said, "Oh Welusa! Welusa, I can't help you, I am not strong enough, but I will find someone that can."

She took off shouting, "Hold on, don't struggle, I'll not be long."

Lianga reassured me saying, "Don't worry Welusa help will come."

I wasn't feeling too hopeful though, because by now I had sunk down up to my arm pits. Then I suddenly remembered the reigns that I got tangled up with. "They must be still in the ditch," I thought.

So I asked Lianga, "Move on slowly Lianga? I think your reigns must be in the ditch behind me."

He then slowly walked on, and as he did so, I felt the reigns brush pass my arm. I grabbed it just as I was sinking even further down. I quickly shouted out, "I've got it! Go on, carry on walking Lianga."

As he did so, I was pulled out of the bog and onto the road to safety.

I lay there and said, "Well done, thank you my friend. You saved me."

He answered, "Not at all Welusa. I did nothing. I only walked on."

I stood up and said, "Phew! That was a bit of luck. I am soaking wet and covered in black peat but I'm going to lie down now in the coach and wait for your queen."

It wasn't long before I heard her sobbing, "Oh no, no Welusa, what have I done again!" I couldn't find anyone. Welusa! Oh Welusa."

I stepped out of the coach and said, "What's all the fuss about? Come on let's go."

She spun around and flung her arms around me saying, "You are safe! Oh Welusa. I uh…"

She was just about to tell me something, when she stopped, frowned and slapped me on my arm, and said, "Oh you, you let me think you were dead, didn't you?"

Lianga laughed and so did I.

"No I didn't," I said.

Then after Lianga told her how I got out, she laughed too.

I swilled my hands and face in a pool of water, washed my boots and changed my clothes. Then set off again.

It stayed foggy all the way until we started to descend down into the city of York. We were happy now to be off those treacherous moors and looking forward to a nice rest and some food.

It was dark when we arrived in the city, so I found a nice little Inn with stables and decided to get a room for the night.

Once again, I must point out to you that whenever we were in contact with anyone, Tianaju, always kept her hood up. This would hide her hair and her beautiful face. I told her to do this because as you can imagine, any man that saw her, would swoon, and likely be a nuisance. We didn't want any unsolicited attention drawn towards us.

We booked a room with two single beds and a stable for Lianga. I asked the Inn keeper, "Could I have a bath please?"

He obliged saying, "Certainly I will prepare one and let you know when it's ready."

We went to the room and collapsed on the beds. "Wow! This is great," I said as I lay there waiting for my bath.

"Hello there. Your bath is ready. The wash room is two rooms away," said the Inn keeper as he knocked on the door.

"Thank you," I shouted back. I took off my jacket and said, "Right I'm off now to have a good soak."

Tianaju coughed and said, "Ah hum but not before me."

I said, "What! You must be joking," and rushed to the washroom to dive in first. Unfortunately by not being a fairy, I lost, because she was there with her bag as soon as I opened the washroom door.

"Ah that's cheating," I told her.

She replied "No, That's magic, so go on hop it. I'll be out in a flash."

I walked out saying, "Ha, ha very funny."

After about fifteen minutes the bedroom door opened and in she came smiling, saying, "Ah, that was nice. Sorry about the water, it's a bit cold now."

I smiled because I knew she was only kidding but I still said, "Yeah, better mind it isn't."

So I took my soap and towel with me and found that I was right. The water was still warm and soapy. I got in and it was lovely, so I stayed there soaking away until it was cold. I got dressed and went back into the bedroom. Tianaju had lit a small fire in the hearth and was drying my boots in front of it. She was sitting alongside the fire looking at me dressed in a long white nightdress and a red robe.

"Where did you get your lovely night wear from? Was it magic?" I asked.

She answered "No, it wasn't magic. Nabalion brought them to me while you were bathing. Come and sit with me by the fire. Tell me which town are we heading for next?"

It was difficult sitting down beside her, trying to remember the name of the town. Every time I looked at her, she looked back at me with those lovely green eyes. She was so mesmerizing sitting there holding my hand that everything I tried to say got all muddled up. In fact, I didn't even know what I was talking about half of the time. She was so beautiful. As for remembering the name of the town it was hopeless. So in the end I gave up and said, "I'll tell you in the morning. Good night I'm off to bed."

"Okay, so will I. Good night. See you in the morning, Welusa."

I tossed and turned for a while until I heard the Town Crier shouting, "It's twelve o'clock and all is well. The taverns are closed and there is no more news to tell."

I turned over once more and fell asleep.

"Good morning," shouted a lady as she knocked on the bedroom door. "Would you like breakfast before you leave?"

I looked over to Tianaju who was dressed and sitting on the bed. She nodded and said, "Yes."

So I shouted, "Yes please, we will be down shortly. Toast is all we need, thank you."

While enjoying our nice warm toast, I still couldn't remember the name of the next town, so I told Tianaju that we were just heading for Scarborough. I settled up with the Inn Keeper, collected Lianga, and away we went heading for the east coast of Scarborough.

The weather was fine for the next few days and there was no sign of the dragon so progress was good. We arrived at a small village with a general store. Tianaju suggested we stop at the store and stock up on things we might need.

I agreed, "Yes, that's a good idea. Come on then, let's tie up Lianga and go inside."

She collected everything she thought we needed, and I paid the lady store keeper five pennies for them. I mentioned to the lady that we were going to Scarborough and asked her how much farther was it that we had to go.

She came from around the counter before answering, "Scarborough is only about a day's ride away. There is a market there tomorrow. Are you going there to sell?"

I replied, "No, we are going there to pass a message on to someone."

She tapped me on the shoulder and said, "Well, in that case, you should call into the market at the same time, because it's the best one in England."

We left the store thanking her and once again carried on our journey. It was still a fine, warm day, as you would expect for the time of year. So as we were trotting along we saw in the distance what appeared to be a man lying in the road and a loose horse. As we drew nearer I could see that he seemed to be in pain. We stopped, climbed down, and rushed over to help him. As we approached him he jumped to his feet wielding a large stick. He grabbed Tianaju and demanded me to give him my money or else she would die.

Tianaju did nothing so I said, "I doubt it but you can have my purse anyway."

I threw the purse on the ground away from him and told him to let her go. He laughed as he did so then picked up the purse and ran to his horse. As he ran the purse changed into a yellow and blue woodpecker. The woodpecker pecked his hand and then his nose. The man yelled with pain and ran away screaming, holding his nose chasing his terrified horse. We laughed as we watched him chase his horse out of sight.

I asked Tianaju, "Why didn't you just disappear?"

She answered, "I just wanted to have some fun, that's all."

The woodpecker had now changed back into my purse again. So I picked it up and put it safely back into my pocket, and said, "I hope we don't meet any more like him today."

Tianaju laughed then assured me saying, "Well if we do, they will get the same treatment."

We then set off again, laughing as we went.
By the time we reached Scarborough it was well after midnight. So we decided to set up camp in the woods on the outskirts of the town. The dragon, once again, was nowhere to be seen. That suited us just fine, as he was such a nuisance. He had probably thought that I was dead in the bog.

In the morning we set out to look for Nipper, the son of the East Wind. We searched the coastline's high rocky cliffs and before long we could hear him whistling and blowing. We ventured further until I saw him standing in a massive cove below the ruins of Scarborough Castle.

He looked just like an enormous mass of frosty spiky stars, with a spiteful face, towering way above the castle. He was facing east, blowing the cold icy North Sea air over to his father the East Wind. I plucked up some courage and began to wave and shout, "Nipper, Nipper down here, I'm down here."

He slowly turned and looked down at me with his piercing icy blue eyes. He then gave me such a fright as he roared and spiraled into the air, thundered across the sea, turned and screamed back towards me. I stood there pretending to be brave as he blasted me with frost, pinning me up against the rocks, saying, "Who are you?" Speak, before I blast you out across the sea."

I answered with a lump in my throat, "I am Welusa. I have come with a serious message from the Emerald Queen of Children. I have already delivered this message to your cousins; Soaker and Toaster. Will you please listen to it? The queen herself is standing over there."

He thought for a minute and roared, "Hah! Do you think I'm a fool?"

I was getting worried now as he held me there peering into my eyes. It seemed for ever before he finally said, "Well you look and sound genuine enough, so let me hear this serious message?"

He then released me and I fell onto the soft sand. I got up and stood there covered in frost, shivering as I relayed the queen's message to him. When I had finished he once again spiraled high into the air, came down and blew all the frost off me, saying "I'll think about it. Now be gone."

With that he hovered back to his cove.

"Do you think he will tell his father Tianaju?" I asked, as I shivered my way over to her.

"Yes, he is just trying to be important that's all," she replied as she rubbed my back and shoulders trying to warm me up.

"Well that's that," I said with a sigh of relief. "One more to go and hopefully they will band together. Come on let's go and check out the market. I'm freezing."

The queen gave me a big hug and promised, "Right, come on I'll buy you something nice."

The market was easy enough to find, because it was in the middle of the town. There were all sorts of stalls selling everything that you might need. Tianaju bought me a lovely thick leather jacket. It was the first one that I had ever had. I put it on to warm me up and continued browsing around the stalls. Suddenly a man shouted out, "There she is! That's her. That's the witch that I was telling you about. Get her!"

Before I could do anything, the man grabbed Tianaju and pulled down her hood. He gasped, along with everyone else that saw her.

I pushed the man away and said, "Quick! Run Tianaju, over to the coach."

We ran to the coach, opened the door and I pushed her in. As I was about to climb up myself, I was dragged back down and held by three men.

I ordered Lianga, "Go! Leave me. Go and hide somewhere."

He spun around and raced off out of town.

"You'll pay for this. Where's that witch gone? Tie him up to that post and whip him. We'll make him talk," shouted the angry man.

I shouted back to him, "I'll tell you nothing, only that she is not a witch, she is my uh, she is my wife."

The man looked me in the face and said, "Well if that's the case, you are a witch too. I heard you talking to that horse. Whip him boys! He'll soon tell us where she's gone."

They tied me to a post and whipped me three times across my legs before someone shouted, "Leave him!"

It was the town Mayor who was crying, "Leave him! Bring him into the court house."

The angry man shouted back, "NO! Hold the mayor boys while I deal with this witch's husband." His gang held back the mayor and as he rose his whip to strike me there was a screaming gust of wind that blew him over. I looked up the street, and there was Nipper making his way down in the shape of a whirlwind, scattering people and stalls everywhere.

If it wasn't for the fact that I was tied to the post, I too, would have been blown away. Nipper, then, with one icy freezing breath, froze the ropes that bound me, and with one more blast, broke them, and I was free.

"Go! Go tell the queen that I have decided to give my father your message. Hurry now, your coach is waiting outside of town."

I thanked him for saving me and ran as fast as I could to get away from those crazy people.

Tianaju and Lianga were waiting just where Nipper had told me they would be. She hugged me and said, "Come on let's get away from here."

I climbed up and said, "Yes! On you go Lianga, as fast as you like. Head north, we are off to Scotland."

As we galloped away I could still hear Nipper screaming behind us. My legs were sore now, but I kept that to myself. I was thankful that Tianaju knew nothing about me being whipped. I only told her about the men tying me up, and how Nipper saved me.

Once again I must point out to you, the reason why Tianaju did not disappear when she was attacked, was because it would have only caused us to be pursued all over the country.

That night, after traveling at least twenty miles, we camped in the woods of Harwood Dale. I made a nice fire with my last bit of flint, and roasted some nice potatoes. As we were enjoying them I looked at Tianaju and told her, "The man that grabbed you in the market was the same man that was lying in the road and robbed us."

She looked at me and said, "Was he?

I replied, "Yes, it must have been him, because he had a red nose, the size of a ripe tomato."

She dropped her potato and burst out laughing and so did I. In fact after supper we lay down with our blankets and laughed ourselves to sleep.

The next part of our journey was very tedious indeed, stopping only to get more flints, rest Lianga and to eat and sleep. We traveled on until we camped, one night, on the outskirts of Morpeth. We were looking up at the clear night sky and although it was the night of a full moon, the moon appeared to be not so bright now.

Tianaju exclaimed, "Look! Look at the moon. Ohibronoeler looks as though he is succeeding with his threat. Oh, I do hope all the winds will help us to get rid of him."

I calmed her down, by assuring her, "Don't worry, the winds will help us. We have done well so far, we must keep faith in what we are doing. Sleep well now, because it's a long journey to Jedburgh tomorrow."

It was foggy as we headed out the following morning. This made me think about the dragon and how long would it be before he discovered I was still alive? We traveled along an old, bumpy road that ran between vast fir trees for most of the journey. The fog stayed with us for a few more days before it lifted. Then our surroundings began to change. We were now following a winding road up a steep mountain side. So reaching the top was tough going for Lianga. On reaching the peak we were met with a beautiful view looking out towards Scotland and back towards England. It was so wonderful that we sat there and took in its magnificence.

Then, to my dismay, I noticed that the dragon was drifting in the sky, heading towards us.

I shouted and pointed, "Look, there he is! It's him. He's seen us."

Before I had even finished speaking, he swooped down upon us saying, "Ah, so you managed to survive the bog Welusa. Ho, ho, you're in trouble now Tianaju. Using your magic eh, helping humans on a mission against me. YES, I have finally got my revenge on your father. He will have no other choice but to strip you of your magic, and banish you from Fairyland. So carry on fools, I'm off. I am feeling a little peckish now, and could do with a few more snacks of those nice juicy moonbeams."

He then soared off into the sky, laughing as he went.

"Take no notice of him," said Tianaju. "I have not helped you in any way. You have done everything yourself. I told you when we started out, that I am only here to keep you company."

I replied, "It's alright, I believe you. He wasn't there when I got out of the bog. So it's Ohibronoeler that is the fool, not us."

I gave her a nudge and said, "Come on, let's see Scotland." Off we went down the mountain road to Jedburgh. We found an Inn, and booked in for the night. There was a room with two beds and a bath for us and a stable for Lianga. The Inn keeper told us that Mary Queen of Scots had once stayed in a house just around the corner. Little did he know that the Emerald Queen of Children would also be staying in Jedburgh that night, and in his very Inn. We were given a very nice cosy room with a small fire. The trip to Jedburgh had really tired us out, so after a bath and supper, we went to our beds and slept all night.

Our next destination was to be Hawick first, then Edinburgh the capital of Scotland. The following morning we headed out on a twisty road, shaded with horse chestnut trees that followed the line of the river. We were only a few miles outside Hawick when we met two distressed young men on the road side. One of them had an arrow in his shoulder and the other was helping him along. I stopped and offered them a lift.

They thanked me and the uninjured one told us, "I am Prince Scott and this is my brother Prince David. I have accidentally shot him while hunting. We would be very grateful if you would take us home. We live with our father King Logan, up there on the hill, in Fatlips Castle."

I asked them, "Where are your horses?"

"We didn't bring our horses," they replied.

Prince Scott and I helped the injured prince into the coach and set off up the hill to the castle. When we arrived there, King Logan was practicing his sword fencing with someone in the castle grounds. On catching sight of us helping Prince David out of the coach, he dropped his sword and rushed over to his sons. Prince Scott told his father what had happened, so he ordered them to go in quickly and get the arrow removed. The king thanked us and insisted we stay the rest of the day and night.

I thanked the king saying, "Thank you for your hospitality, but we really must be on our way."

The king raised his voice and insisted, "You will stay! You will stay and eat with us. I will have Catherine, my house keeper, prepare a room for you. John my cook will make us up a nice meal. Come, you will be my honoured guests. My stable lad, Paul, will see to your fine horse and coach."

Reluctantly, we had no option but to follow the king, with our belongings, into the fascinating castle. As we entered the castle Tianaju let down her hood. The king called out to Catherine asking her to prepare a room for us. Then when he turned around and saw Tianaju he was astonished, just like everyone else before him.

74

"My word laddie, you have a fine wee lassie for a wife," he remarked.

I explained to him that she wasn't my wife; I was just helping her find someone.

He then shouted out again, "Catherine! It's two rooms, not one."

During the day the king took us to the top of his castle and told us, "The town you can see in the distance is Hawick. Hawick is famous for their youth. In the year of fifteen hundred and fourteen they banned together, and defeated an English raiding party that was camped at Hornshole just outside of town. They captured the English flag and paraded it through the town in triumph."

Before he could tell us any more a gong sounded. The king informed us that dinner must be ready. So we made our way down behind him to the great hall. There was a big roaring fire in the hearth, and standing each side of it was Prince Scott and the wounded Prince David. Also lying alongside it was a tan and white hound. The two princes looked at Tianaju and were sent into a daze for a moment, before Prince Scott said, "Welcome friends, it looks like a lovely meal."

The food was well prepared on a large dark oak table. The king asked everyone to sit and enjoy the meal. So we did and it was just as the prince said, a lovely meal. Tianaju and I tried everything bar the rabbit stew.

After dinner the king clapped his hands and shouted, "Bring in Enda the juggler."
We watched as Enda tossed three skittles into the air. He started off in front of us and finished up in the hall way across the room. We were all laughing as we

watched him drop every single one of them. The disgusted king roared, "GET OUT YA FOOL, BEFORE I SET THE DOG ON YE!"

We were later entertained with music and dancing.

Tianaju loved to dance so she asked me, "Shall we have a dance, Welusa?"

I explained to her, "I'm not very good at dancing, but okay, I'll give it a go."

I was happy that I did, because it was great fun. We enjoyed it so much that we danced until we were worn out.

After a lovely entertaining evening we were shown to our rooms. My bed looked lovely and soft and there was a sheep skin rug beside it. I got changed and climbed into bed. It was great.

I was barely asleep for five minutes when I got a poke in the back. I turned around and Tianaju was standing there pointing towards the sheepskin rug.

I asked her, "What's the matter? You have your own bed."

She answered, "I don't like it in that room. It's too creepy."

So I climbed out, got a blanket and led on the rug. I lay there thinking about that nice soft bed and could have cried.

She looked over and asked, "Is the sheepskin soft, Welusa?"

I replied, "Yeah, it's lovely. You should try it."

She turned over, sighed and said, "No this is nicer."

She turned back and looked at me again and said, "I've worked out the name you gave me at Ragged Castle."

I said, "Oh yeah, well the next time I might call you, Pat Sebed."

"That sounds a nice name," she replied.

It wasn't long before I got a gentle clout with a pillow as she said; "I've worked that one out too." I wished her, "Good night, and try to sleep well."

She replied, "Good night I'll try. Thank you for dancing with me."

I said, "It's okay, I enjoyed it."

While lying there with my hands behind my head, I began thinking. "What's going to happen, after we have hopefully defeated the dragon? What am I going to do when she's gone? Wow, that's going to be tough." I sighed, turned over and drifted off to sleep.

In the morning after breakfast we thanked King Logan for his hospitality and wished Prince David a speedy recovery. We thanked our lucky stars that we didn't partake of the rabbit stew, as the king, the princes, the stable lad and the cook who was also the gardener were sick all night.

We all waved goodbye to one another, as we trotted down the hill, and out onto the road heading for Edinburgh. We didn't go through the town of Hawick. Instead we cut across country to Selkirk then Innerleithen. After that it was up and over heather covered mountains to Edinburgh. It took us three more days to reach there. Each night we watched the dragon swallow up as many moonbeams as he could. Tianaju told me, that it would take about six more months, before the dragon would eventually devour them all. We were less than three hundred miles away from Howler, the son of the mighty North wind, so all bar a catastrophe we were not too worried.

The days went by and as we were approaching the outskirts of Edinburgh we were told not to go into the city, as there was a battle going on. We could smell the gunpowder from where we were stood.

As you know, in a battle cannon balls fly everywhere, so we were very fortunate to be warned in time.

So we moved on, heading for Dunkeld, and set up camp for the night in some woods on the way. We mostly camped in woods because it was safer there, hidden away from robbers.

After lighting a fire, we each had a roast potato with melted cheese, and some hot soup. Lianga once again wandered off through the woods. Tianaju told me that we could all do with a rest and suggested we stay a few days in Dunkeld. I agreed, and we went to sleep very happy that night.

It was lovely waking up thinking, "Once we reach Dunkeld there will be no more traveling for a day or two. We are just going to relax and go for walks."

It was a lovely breezy day when we arrived there the following week. We quickly found a nice spot alongside a river, and camped close to a bridge that went over it. On the other side of the river, was a forest with lots of interesting walks, so it was an ideal place to stay.

Before we sat down by the river, the beautiful queen put on a dark green dress with a white sash around her waist and her tiny shrunken wand poking out over it. She never went anywhere without it. She put a white shawl around her shoulders, and had decided not to cover her hair. We were not going to worry about people staring at us. I only had two sets of similar types of clothes, so I just changed into the clean set. Tianaju always insisted on washing my clothes and had done this from the very first day we started out.

We sat on the bank of the river chatting away for most of the morning. Doing nothing for a change was absolutely wonderful. It was so peaceful sitting there listening to the rippling river and watching it flowing along.

I gazed at the sky and said, "It looks like it is going to stay fine Tianaju. Would you like to take a walk through the woods later?"

She answered, "Yes, I would like that very much."

So after lunch we went over the bridge and followed a wide path through the forest, but we were not the only ones taking a walk that day. There were other couples walking in front of us, some of them were with children. It reminded me of every warm Sunday evening back in my home town, when probably half the town folk would walk as couples and friends down Cwmavon road and back.

As we walked along chatting away Tianaju told me, "Further on, we will come to a homemade cave. Some say a blind hermit by the name of Ossian lived there, long before I was born."

When we got to the cave, it was well made and very interesting. If what they say is true, a blind man, living in amongst this forest of tall trees, would have found it extremely difficult to survive.

On the way back, we messed around by throwing a stick each into another but smaller river that was flowing beside the path. We then ran down past four trees, to see whose stick came first. I fell over once, as we raced, and it made her laugh. When we had finished, my score was three and her score was five. She had beaten me fair and square.

As I had fallen over earlier, I felt for my purse and found it was gone. We backed tracked to where it had happened and were just in time to see a jackdaw taking it up to her nest in a tree at the edge of the river. Before we could call out to her she flew away.

"It's okay I'll get it back," said the laughing queen. I insisted, "No, I like climbing trees, I'll fetch it."

The nest was out on a branch so I climbed the tree easily enough, shinned across the branch and collected my purse. As I was shinning back, I slipped and fell, landing head first into a deep pool.

"Wow!" I said, as I came to the surface.

Tianaju stood there laughing saying, "I thought you said you were good at climbing trees?"

I swam out and told her, "Yes I am, I just wanted to show you that I could dive as well."

She laughed and said, "Well it wasn't very good."

I flicked some water over her and she backed away laughing. So I caught her, picked her up, went over to the pool and joked, "Well let's see how good you can dive then?"

"Don't you dare throw me in," she squealed.

So I put her down and said, "Well, I might."

She pushed me away and laughed. We then walked back to the coach discussing what we were going to have for supper.

I joked with her saying, "Well, we could have: tattoes, spuds or tatties."

She replied, "Well, I think I'll have potatoes instead."

So that's what we had and then we went to bed dreaming of potatoes all night long.

We went for another walk and a picnic the following day. On our way back to the camp, after the picnic, Tianaju decided to play a guessing game.

When it was my turn I asked her, "Guess what we are having for supper?"

She laughed and answered, "Well, I'll tell you what we're not having, and that's potatoes because there aren't any left. As soon as we get back, we are off into town for fresh supplies."

So that's exactly what we did. On our way back it was such a lovely warm evening that I suggested, "Shall we stop for a jug of lemonade in the tavern at the edge of the village? I noticed earlier, that there are tables outside. We could sit there and watch the birds go to bed."

She agreed saying, "Yes, it would be nice, that would finish off our lovely few days here in Dunkeld."

We arrived at the tavern and Tianaju sat outside while I fetched the lemonades. It was pleasant sitting there sipping our drinks, watching the birds flying back into the trees to sleep.

Then, out of the corner of my eye I noticed a wobbly man. It was obvious that he had too many jars of the fine ale. He was stood talking to a tall grey haired man.

As I watched, the tall man shouted, "I can't understand a word you are saying. Go away and leave me alone."

Then much to my disappointment the wobbly man turned, caught sight of us, and headed our way.

"Oh no, he is coming to talk to us now. Keep calm I'll think of something," I anxiously said.

He came over and flopped down beside me and started to ask a lot of questions. So I decided to pretend that I couldn't speak English. So I answered him saying, "Hib dabbly bobbly doo."

He said, "What?"

I said, "Hab snibbly snap un shooby."

He said, "Uh! Are you from Germany?"

I carried on with strange signs and said, "Broo abon, dooby dub, un dribble."

By this time Tianaju couldn't hold her laughter any longer. She got up and rushed around the corner. I heard her burst out with laughter which made it very difficult for me to keep a straight face. The drunken man continued asking, "Are you French? Are you Italian? You must be Danish? What about Turkish then?"

Each time I answered him by saying the same old rubbish. In the end, I couldn't stick it any longer. So I just made a sign with my hands, and said, "Shuella bib un snib," then got up and joined the laughing Tianaju around the corner. As we ran away we heard him shout, "It's okay, I'm Irish."

What we had for supper that night I just can't remember. All I can remember is we fell asleep laughing.

In the morning we packed everything away and started out. As we rode through Dunkeld, we saw the same wobbly man, talking to someone else. Once again, the person he was talking to looked as if he was trying to get away.

I said to Tianaju, "He must have been talking all night. Go on Lianga, before he sees us. Let's head north, to find Howler."

We were thankful that we had two lovely days, as it had now started to rain. It was not a problem to us until we were swamped by the dreaded dragon again.

He snarled at me saying, "So, you still won't listen to me, Welusa. You're a crazy fool. She is playing with your heart to protect her evil father. I begged and pleaded with him not to be cruel to the lovely innocent fairies. I too am innocent, Welusa. Help me get back to myself. Take her wand and give it to me, then I will reward you with greatness. She will give you nothing, only a broken heart. She did the same thing to me. After I helped her find the thief who stole her crystal, she spat in my face, then flew away laughing. She left me weeping, desperately crying out for her. Believe me Welusa, I sobbed and sobbed more than any man alive. So what do you say? Will you help me?"

I waited for a while before I answered him, saying, "I thought you told her that she would be banished from Fairyland, and that you had won. You also told us that you weren't bothered any more about us. Hah! I can see your boots shivering from here. Go away and sob some more."

He was enraged once again and roared out, "YOU HAVE OFFENDED ME WELUSA! Before the week is out you will wish that you had never set eyes on your pretty deceiver."

With that, he sprayed us with some slimy water, and took off to the east.

"Well that put pay to him, Tianaju," I said as I wiped the slimy stuff off us.

"Yes, and a good riddance too," she replied.

Both of us were relieved to see him go. Plus we had a clear view now to make better progress.

Our encounters with Ohibronoeler lasted for another week which delayed our journey badly. So we only got as far as just outside a village called Killie Crankie.

We came alongside a lodge, just before a bridge over a fast running river. We stopped and Tianaju knocked on the door and a kind looking lady answered.

"Could you please spare us a jug of water?" asked Tianaju.

"Certainly, the pump is around the side," replied the lady. "Have you traveled far?" she asked.

Tianaju answered, "Yes, we have traveled hundreds of miles, and are now heading for the north coast."

The lady took Tianaju's hand and said, "My poor dear, you and your husband must be exhausted. Why don't you stay here with me for the night? I live on my own and your company will be most welcome. I have a nice pot of broth on the fire and a nice warm bed in my spare room. My name is Priscilla, but you can call me Cilla, put your horse in the stable around the back."

Tianaju didn't tell her that I was not her husband because she only had one spare room.

We accepted Cilla's offer, unhitched Lianga, gave him his oats and bedded him down for the night. After gathering our bags, Priscilla put them in our bedroom. We then sat around her table and enjoyed a nice bowl of Scotch broth. Later, it was nice chatting to one another in front of a cosy fire.

Cilla even sang a few Scottish songs for us, and for an elderly lady, she had a lovely voice.

After her last song she said, "Well I better let you go to bed. You are tired and so am I."

We wished her good night, and she wished us the same. As usual Tianaju slept in the nice comfy bed, and I slept on the floor.

We slept until Priscilla called us for breakfast. After we enjoyed a nice warm bowl of porridge, Cilla gave Tianaju a loaf of bread and some cheese to pack in her bag. The queen thanked her and promised that she will never be forgotten.

We crossed over the bridge and onto the road leading north. On each side of this road were large mountains that were going on for miles. We traveled on for about an hour or so. Ahead of us now was a sky full of black looking rain clouds. As we approached them, it began to rain, which turned into a terrible thunder and lightning storm. There was nothing we could do, only stop on the road side and wait for it to pass. Lianga was restless, so I put on the brake and chocks, and unhitched him from the coach. I was so happy that I did, because what happened later was something I had never witnessed before in my life. The storm did not stop, instead it worsened. The river, alongside of us, began to rise. Then the exasperated Tianaju held my arm and pointed, "Look! The mountain is moving."

I looked, and couldn't believe my eyes. On the other side of the river the whole side of the mountain was rapidly sliding towards us.

"It's a landslide!" Lianga shouted. "Quick! Jump up onto my back. I will take you to safety."

I grabbed our bags, and we leaped onto Lianga's strong back. Within a minute, we were galloping up the other mountain side, away from a terrible death. The land slide had swamped the river, ripping up trees and anything else that was in its way. We watched as our lovely coach got smashed by one of the trees then disappeared into a swamp of mud and rubble. After the storm had ceased there was a raging flood. The road was nonexistent now in fact the whole area for as far as you could see was just a sea of mud, rubble and floating trees. It was a devastating sight.

I was soaking wet and so was Tianaju. I asked her, "Why don't you use your wand and dry yourself?"

She answered, "No, I have been trying to suffer along with you on this journey. It is the least I can do."

No matter how many times I asked her, she still refused to dry herself.

In the end I said, "Okay if that's what you want, put my blanket around you."

I took my blanket out of my bag, and put it around her shivering shoulders. It was not long before the sun came out and we began to dry off.

While we were sitting on the hillside watching the flood, Lianga nudged me and said, "Don't worry Welusa. Come on both of you, up onto my back. Let's head on."

The queen looked at me and asked, "What do you think?"

I answered, "Well, what are we waiting for? Come on, my beautiful bonnie lass, let's go and finish it."

She hugged my arm and said, "You are up front because I need to hold on."

I smiled and said, "That suits me fine."

Away we went, slowly across the side of the mountain. I had no reigns to hold onto, but Lianga had a broad back and his mane was long. So I was safe enough, holding on to his mane. We made steady progress until we heard the roaring sound of water in the distance. It was a raging river running through a gully, and the almost deafening sound of water was coming from a waterfall crashing down into a massive muddy pool. The river then flowed on down to the valley below. It was impossible for us to cross this gully. So the only thing to do was to go up river, find a narrow place to cross and wait until the river subsides.

It was dusk before Lianga found a narrow part of the river, but it was still raging and un-crossable. We had no coach now so I had to think of how we were going to bed down for the night.

I suggested, "If we spread a blanket onto a nice soft patch of heather and pull up large piles of them, we can stack them around us. What do you think?"

The queen answered, "That sounds good, as long as it doesn't rain again. It will help keep the cold night breeze from us."

This is what we did and it worked well. Tianaju took Priscilla's loaf of bread and cheese out of her bag, and we had our well-earned supper.

Later she informed me, "As I was watching the thunder storm I saw the dragon, swallowing up streaks of its lightening. I think Ohibronoeler is saving these to use as a weapon. If you can remember, he once told us that he had a plan."

I replied, "Yes, I remember."

She continued, "Well, I am sure this is part of it. He must be collecting them from all around the world. He knows that thunder and lightning is the only thing the winds do not like. It badly weakens them momentarily."

I led down and said, "Come on, lie down beside me, don't worry, we'll get him."

She lay down and we covered ourselves with two blankets. Without thinking, I put my arm around her and immediately pulled it away, saying, "Oh, I'm sorry, I just forgot myself."

She replied as she pulled my arm back, "It's okay, I don't mind, you are nice and warm."

So that's how I stayed for most of the night, until Nabalion came and spoiled it.

He relayed a message from her father saying, "Obibronoeler has swallowed up, most of the moonbeams from the southern and western part of the world. As a result there are many stranded fairies there unable to come back home. He wants you and I to rescue them before it's too late."

She looked at me with her lovely caring eyes and asked, "Will you be alright here on your own, Welusa?"

I replied, "Yes, of cause I will. Don't worry about me, I will be fine. Go and save those poor kind fairies. The river will surely take a day or two to calm down. Lianga and I will sit here and wait until then."

I lifted her up onto Nabalion saying, "Go on then, hurry. I'll still be here when you get back."

She caught hold of my hand and said, "Welusa, I, er I, or never mind, just be careful that's all." Nabalion soared into the night sky and they disappeared out of sight.

It was still a chilly night so I led back down. Lianga had wandered off in search of grass because his oats were swept away in the flood. I tossed and turned a while before falling asleep.

I wasn't asleep for long before I was awakened by a deep voice saying, "BOO."

It was the thick, misty, hairy tormenting Ohibronoeler. He was all frosted up. His breath was cold and icy, and he wasn't looking very pleased.

He spoke in a sarcastically slow nasty voice, "Welusa, where's your pretty, poochy, woochy, girly friend gone? Is she gone to save her fairy wairies? Dear, dear, what a shame, she'll never find them. I've got them all in my bin, Ha! She will never come back, because she will never find them. What do you think of that, yah old fool Welusa?"

I sat up and just laughed at him saying, "She is only gone to have her hair done, and to freshen up. She is also fetching some strawberries and cream for later on. So go away with your fiby wiby liesy wiseys before she smacks your potty, totty spotty botty."

His eyes turned red with anger as he growled at me saying, "You think you're very clever sonny. How dare you laugh at me? Well, you'll laugh at me no more. In fact you'll never laugh again."

He then breathed his icy cold breath all over me. I began to feel so numb that I couldn't move. He continued with his smelly frosty breath, until I could feel myself beginning to pass out.

He shouted, "NO! Not yet, dear Welusa, not before you feel my awesome power."

I noticed, as he stretched out his long misty, hairy fingers, that they were covered in frost. He began to run them slowly over me, saying, "You are going to die Welusa, just like I promised. If your sweet heart returns, all she'll find is a block of ice. I will wipe out the winds, smash Fairyland, get back my wand, and build a new land of my own."

As he ran his freezing cold fingers over my body, he suddenly screamed out with pain. As he backed away holding his hand I could see that it was now a small real fleshy red dragon's claw. At the same time there was a flash, and from his claw came a shower of sparkles streaming towards the moon. I could now feel my shirt pocket beginning to get very warm. All I could think of was, when he touched my pocket, his long horrid hairy hand changed into a red blooded claw, the size of my hand. He then took off heading north screaming as he went.

Lianga, who had heard the screams, came to my aid. He realised what the dragon had done and began to breathe his warm breath all over me. As I slowly began to feel myself again, I sank back onto the heather thanking him. I looked at my pocket and found that it was open and so was my pouch. The horrible dragon must have tried to take it.

It was quite some time before I fully recovered, and I was very thankful when the sun rose. It warmed me up, making me feel a lot better.

The river had receded now but was still not crossable. The reason for this was the main river had to make its way around the huge landslide down the valley, before the gully river could once more flow freely again.

It took four days of sunshine and dry nights before we were able to cross it. On the morning that we crossed the river, which was now running clear, I said to Lianga, "We will wait here until the queen returns. In the meantime I will have to make some kind of shelter."

There were plenty of stones that had been washed up onto the river bank, so this gave me an idea. I slowly collected them and began to build a small cabin. It was about six feet long and three feet wide. I made one side about four feet tall and the other side a foot shorter.

I collected ferns for the roof. Unfortunately there were only a few sticks around to support the ferns so it took some time to layer them in a fashion to make it reasonably water proof.

When I had finished, Lianga remarked, "Well done, Welusa. That's a fine shelter." Then, he jokingly asked, "But what about me?"

I replied, "Well, you could probably squash a bit of yourself in, just as long as it isn't your tail end."

He laughed and trotted away saying, "I'm off for a snack, see you later cabin boy."

Later, as I sat on the bank watching the river twisting its way down through the wide gully, my pocket began to tingle. I quickly got to my feet and spun around. There, sitting on Nabalion, still wearing her traveling clothes, was my beautiful, smiling Emerald Queen of Children. I didn't give her time to dismount. I rushed over and gently lifted her down and said, "Wow, if ever I have missed anyone in my life, it's you. I am so happy to see you again. You took our bread and cheese away with you. Have you got any left because I'm starving?"

She pushed me away and said, "Oh you! You're teasing me again aren't you?

I smiled at her and said, "Yes I am, but I have missed you though."

She smiled back and warned me, "Better mind you are telling me the truth."

Lianga had seen her coming, and came trotting up. "Hello your Majesty, are the fairies safe and well?" he asked.

She replied, "Yes they are."

Nabalion then added, "You are doing a magnificent job Lianga. We are all proud of you."

He thanked Nabalion, "I am only too happy to serve Her Majesty and Fairyland."

Nabalion bowed his head and backed away saying, "I must leave you now, your Highness."

He then turned, and gracefully soared into the air and was gone.

Tianaju and Nabalion are some of the very few that are able to fly in and out of Fairyland, day or night, without the need of moonbeams.

Later, I asked Tianaju, "Are you too tired to move on? Or would you like to rest here and head out tomorrow?"

She answered, "No, I am not tired, I'll be happy to do whatever you think is best."

I thought for a while and said, "The weather is fine now, so I think we should head on. We need to get off this mountain and back onto the road. That is if we can find it. Hopefully we can purchase a tent in the next village, or maybe buy some material to make one. What do you think?"

The queen replied, "That's a good idea. I'm ready when you are."

I looked at my cabin and said quietly to myself, "Well, that was a waste of time building, but it doesn't matter; it might come in handy for someone else."

So we collected our bags, mounted Lianga, and he walked off through the heather. We trekked on following a goat's path that was heading across and down the mountain. We were making good headway until Lianga strayed off the track to grab a mouthful of grass. Then, without warning he veered sharply to the left, causing Tianaju and I to slip off and fall onto the heather. As we were getting up I grabbed Tianaju and held her up in my arms. There in front of us, curled up on a rock about four feet away, was an adder, ready to strike. I slowly moved backwards until I was back on the track safely away from it.

Tianaju's face was as white as snow now as she looked at me saying, "Oh, I don't like snakes."

"Neither do I," I told her as she held her arms around my neck. "Come on, let's get from here. The quicker we get back onto the road, the better it will be."

Lianga apologised, "I am so sorry my queen the snake gave me such a fright."

She replied, "It's okay. Come on let's go."

Within about two seconds we were up on his back, and raced away like three scared rabbits, down the mountain and onto the road. It was such a relief when we finally reached the road that we started laughing. We were laughing because we were so happy to be off that mountain.

It was time to move on now to the next village for fresh supplies. Lianga walked at a steady pace until we were stopped by a tramp on the roadside. He said his name was Chris and that he had been in this country working ever since he had left Canada a year ago.

He informed me saying, "I am on my way to Glasgow to work my fare on board a ship back home to Canada. I have had enough of tramping around working here and there, sending money back home to my family. So I am looking forward to being with them again, especially my Grandnippers. I lost my tent and belongings in the flood. So I was wondering do you have a spare tent that I could have?"

I answered, "No, but up there on the hillside is a nice cabin that should keep you dry and warm for a while."

I remembered to point out to him that there were snakes up there, but as long as he keeps to the path they won't bother him.

He thanked me and said, "I'll nip up and take a look." He then asked, "Where are you going?"

I replied, "To the next village. Can you tell me how far it is please?"

Chris answered, "It's Carrbridge and it's about two days of walking."

We thanked him and walked on as he headed up the hillside to the cabin.

It clouded over later and began to rain on and off for the next two days. We were soaking wet now so I decided to stop at a small cottage to ask my way. I knocked on the door and a middle aged couple answered.

"Hello there laddie," said a smiling gentleman.

I let down my hood and asked, "I am sorry to trouble you, Sir, but could you please tell me how much farther it is to Carrbridge?"

He answered, "It's just down the road lad."

I then asked him if there was an Inn there.

The lady replied, "No, there is no Inn, only a store. Carrbridge is just a hamlet."

She caught sight of Tianaju sitting up on Lianga and was shocked. She put her hands to her face and said, "Dear me, your young wife looks worn out and pure drenched to the bone. If you are looking for somewhere to stay, you are welcome to use our barn. I have some clothes that you can wear, while I dry yours by the fire."

We were very grateful to them and accepted their hospitality. It was ideal, because Lianga could shelter there too. We went into the barn that was half full of hay, and waited for the lady. It wasn't long before she came in with some dry clothes and two towels to dry us with.

She told us, "My name is Patricia and my husband's name is Stuart. Bring your wet clothes in and I will make you a wee bowl of hot soup. You must be perished, lass."

We changed and took our wet clothes over to her.

"I'll put them by the fire later," she said.

Then she called out, "Stuart! Warm up that nice pot of soup for us love."

Stuart when he saw Tianaju remarked, "My word lass, you are the bonniest lassie I've ever seen in my life."

He then looked at me and said, "Why, you must be the luckiest lad alive to have such a beautiful wife."

I was just about to tell him that she wasn't my wife, when I said to myself, "If I tell them she's not, they might not let us stay." So I just told them our names and where we were going.

Stuart said "Well lad, if that's where you're heading, you will need warmer clothes than the ones you were wearing. It's possible the store in the village may have what you need. Now until the soup is ready, would you like a mug of ale or a wee dram of whiskey lad?"

I replied "No, no thank you."

"Well what about the wife then? Would she like a wee dram?"

I replied, "No thank you, she doesn't like it."

He replied, "Well in that case I'll just have a wee sup myself before we enjoy our soup and my homemade bread."

The soup was lovely and warm and so was the fire. It was a shame we had to leave it. Before we left, we offered to wash up the dishes but Patricia insisted, "No, no, no Stuart will do them later."

So we wished the kind couple good night and went back to the barn. I took out our blankets, which were kept dry in our leather bags, and lay them on the hay. Tianaju led down and I covered her with a blanket making sure she was snug and cosy. I lay down and decided to tell her what Ohibronoeler had done to me while she was away.

When I mentioned how his hand changed as it crept over my pocket, she sat up saying, "That's it!

It's my lock of hair. It must have affected him. I wonder why? What do you think Welusa?"

We sat there deep in thought until she remembered and said, "When Ohibronoeler captured me I had no magic powers. Therefore my hair was normal the time he used it to change himself into the horrid dragon. So when his hand came into contact with my magic lock of hair, it caused a reaction. This reaction somehow changed it into a real dragon's claw, releasing some of the moonbeams."

I pondered for a moment then gave her my thoughts, "If it is anything to do with your hair, the dragon would have reacted to it earlier. Remember, for most of our journey he has been smothering us. Not only did I have the lock of your hair in my pocket, you also have a full head of magic hair yourself. So why didn't it affect him then?"

We led back down in thought for a while. Then both of us sat up again saying together, "It's the icy frost. When he was in his frosty form, the magic hair changed his hand to a real dragon's claw."

Then we slumped back down again saying, "But why?"

We lay there deep in thought again until Tianaju sat up excitedly saying, "I think I know the answer. Ever since my terrible time in Apsinider I have hated the cold. So the instant reaction of my magic hair would be to turn his freezing, hairy dragon's hand, into a warm blooded one. So because Ohibronoeler was in the form of a dragon it turned it into a claw."

We were so pleased with our selves for solving the mystery that we hugged one another.

"Yes! We've got him!" I exclaimed, as I nearly kissed her forehead. Once again I immediately apologised. I told her I was just excited that we had found something to use against him.

She said, "That's okay, I am excited too."

As we led back down my mind was working overtime thinking of a plan. Eventually I came up with one. The plan was for the four winds to bring him together and hold him in this state long enough to frost him up. If I could then somehow toss Tianaju's lock of hair into the frosted dragon, hopefully this would turn him into a warm blooded one, releasing all the moonbeams as he shrinks. How I would be able to toss the hair, I didn't know. I would have to ask the winds.

Tianaju thought it sounded like a good plan but I would have to toss it into the middle where his heart is.

I thought for a while then asked, "If I remember correctly you told me that Ohibronoeler had only been the dragon for a few months?"

She replied, "Yes why?"

I replied, "Well that means you gave me the lock of your hair in good faith, not knowing that one day I would be sent on a mission of destruction. Therefore it belongs to me and I can do what I like with it. So when I use it against the dragon it will have nothing to do with you. Thus my beautiful Queen you will be safe."

"Yes! You're a genius Welusa. Thank you. You have him now," she said excitedly.

So we both led down and went to sleep very happy.

In the morning, Patricia gave us back our dry clothes and asked us in for some breakfast. They had already had theirs, so while we were having ours Stuart went out into the barn. After breakfast we stayed around the table chatting to Patricia, until Stuart came in saying, "Well, that's done. Your fine horse now has a new set of shoes for your travel."

Patricia smiled and informed us saying, "Stuart was a Blacksmith years ago. He told me last night that he was going to give Lianga a new set of shoes."

We thanked Stuart for doing that for him and thanked the both of them for letting us stay.

As we trotted away Tianaju shouted, "I will never forget you."

Stuart shouted back, "You are welcome to call in on your way back."

We stopped at the village store and bought some; food, milk, flints, and soap. We didn't buy oats for Lianga because we had nowhere to put them. I asked the store man if he had any tents or some material to make one.

He replied, "I have none lad, but what I do have is an old tent, with no sticks or pegs."

I told him that will do, and spent my last penny on it.

He asked me, "Where are you heading?"

I replied, "We are going to Inverness."

He warned us, "Be careful crossing our village bridge. The last flood we had, destroyed the parapets on it. So go easy and cross over one at a time."

As the three of us walked towards the bridge, I mentioned, "Well, that's me out of money now. We only have enough food for a few days, but by then we should have accomplished our mission."

Tianaju informed me, "It's okay, we have more than enough. I still have quite a lot of cheese, and apples left."

We walked one after another over the battered bridge, mounted Lianga and galloped away across the mountain road, leaving Carrbridge behind us.

Inverness was about four hours away, and the weather was hot and sunny. Riding Lianga was completely different from sitting on a coach, so we rested more often. It was late afternoon before we stopped for the rest of the day in a large forest of oak trees, near Inverness.

The trees were shading us nicely from the sun. So I cut a couple of straight staffs and sticks and set up the old tent. After I had erected it Tianaju lit a small fire to make supper and we chatted until the sun went down. A number of night birds visited us throughout the evening, telling us that the dragon was not only collecting moonbeams, he was also devouring thunder and lightning. This, we already knew, but we thanked them anyway. Then a beautiful tawny owl with lovely big eyes came floating down.

"Welusa, my name is Angela I come from the Groves. We owls have been studying the dragon for some time now and have worked out his routine. He is collecting the moonbeams using the same pattern throughout the world. During the next full moon he will be passing through the middle of Scotland."

We both thanked the lovely owl and she went away very pleased with herself.

It was time to bed down now, so we wished each other good night. We must have only been asleep for an hour when I heard Lianga calling me. He was warning me that there was a wolf prowling around us. I sat up hearing him warning me again. I put on my jacket and crawled slowly out from the tent. The fire had gone out so there was nothing to frighten him away with, so I grabbed my spare staff and waited. To make matters worse the fog had come down over night. Thankfully it was not the dragon, just highland mist.

"Welusa, he's over there by the twin trees. I have been watching him sneaking around for a while. He looks angry and could be very dangerous," warned Lianga.

I suddenly remembered that I was able to speak to him, but before I had the time to tell him that we were friends he came rushing out from the fog, running straight for me. I pointed my staff towards him and as he sprang through the air I flicked him to one side, sending him crashing into the dead fire. I backed away and he attacked again. I waited until he sprang and flicked him in exactly the same way. This time I heard him yelp as he crashed in to a tree.

I could not see him now so all I could think of was to call out, "Whoa, whoa I am your friend."

It wasn't long before he came in again. This time he was very crafty and came in low and slow. He was snarling now, and creeping slowly towards me. I could see that he was an elderly wolf and most of his teeth were missing and broken. As he crept nearer, I told him once again that I was his friend, but I could see in his savage eyes that he wasn't listening to me. He then ran towards me, so I swung my staff but completely missed him. Before I could swing again he had knocked me to the ground. The next second he had my left arm clamped in his jaws. If it wasn't for my leather jacket he would have torn my arm to pieces. As we rolled over I tried to grab his throat but he just kept shaking my arm and dragging me around. The force of his crushing jaws was so powerful they were painfully deadening my arm. As we wrestled, I realised I was now fighting for my life because he was taking no notice of my pleas. Everything was happening so fast and when you are fighting for your life with no weapon you do the strangest things. So as we rolled around wrestling, somehow I managed to bite his ear close to his head, and dug my strong nails into his tender belly. I squeezed with all the strength that I had left. He loosed go of my arm and yelped out in pain. He was now struggling, trying to twist around to get at my neck and shoulder, then my other arm. No matter how much he struggled I didn't lose go of his ear or his belly. It was a terrible frightening sound as we rolled over and over with him screaming in pain, snarling and growling. He was kicking and scratching desperately trying to get at my shoulder and arm. How I managed to keep him pinned down I will never know. In the end, he gave out a continuous cry that made me realise that he was giving up. It sounded like he wanted to get away from me and the pain. I still held on to him until he gave out such a dreadful pitiful cry that I took a chance and loosed him go. I then quickly got up and backed away. Immediately he did the same and thankfully limped away, back into the forest whimpering and shaking his head.

I spat out a mouthful of hair just before Tianaju rushed over to help me take off my jacket and shirt. My arm was bleeding and down from my elbow to the ends of my fingers were numb. The top side of my arm had deep gashes in it, from the wolf dragging me around, but underneath was just bruised. Fortunately for me he was an old wolf with broken and missing bottom teeth. My side and stomach were covered in scrapes and bruises from the wolf's nails. It felt as if I had been burned with a hot iron.

"Oh Welusa you are bleeding everywhere! We must do something to stop it," the queen said anxiously.

I was worried now thinking that the wolf might have rabies. So what I did next was either right or wrong, I didn't know, but it was the only thing that I could think of.

"Can you make a fire?" I asked her. "I need to try and clean these wounds on my arm, just in case the wolf has rabies."

She quickly lit a fire then asked me sympathetically, "What can I do for you now?"

I replied, "All I want you to do is, go inside the tent and stay there. Don't come out until I tell you to."

I waited for her to go inside before I picked up a burning stick from the fire then blew it out. I then picked up one of the pegs I made for the tent and placed it between my teeth, and bit on it hard.

Placing the red hot stick on my five gashes was about the hardest thing I have ever done. Tianaju heard my muffled cries and came crawling out.

She apologised to me saying, "Oh Welusa! I am so sorry I couldn't help you. I can't use…"

Before she could say any more I put my good arm around her and said, "I know! Please don't cry, I hate to see you sad. I'm okay, he's gone now."

My wounded arm was starting to come back to life now and I was beginning to feel the pain.

"Let me see what I can do with it," she said as she tenderly supported my arm.

I managed to joke, "I hope you are not going to try and kiss it better?"

She replied, "No, but I would if I could."

Together with some moss, chopped up leaves from some kind of shrub, and a strip from one of her dresses, she gently bandaged my arm and said, "There, that's the best I can do."

There was nothing much she could do for my scrapes and bruises only to bath them.

I was so tired and in so much pain that it was almost impossible for me to sleep. But eventually when I did manage to drop off, the queen let me sleep until breakfast time. She then brewed me up a cup of fine herbal tea to ease my aches and pains.

I thanked her and suggested, "We should pack up, go into Inverness, and find a way to cross its river."

She was worried about my arm and wanted me to rest a few days. I assured her that I would be okay and that we should press on. My arm was painfully throbbing now and my hand and fingers had swollen up but I wasn't going to let it stop me. We packed up and headed into Inverness to find a ford to cross the river. I asked Lianga to walk slowly, not to trot, because of my arm. When we entered the town it was market day and extremely busy. There were stalls selling everything from buttons to cattle. I dismounted Lianga and told him to stay there with the queen. If there was any trouble, they must run away and wait.

I walked slowly through the market asking a few people where the nearest ford was. Unfortunately none of them could understand me. I walked on until I noticed an elderly friar who was just purchasing a brown and white nanny goat. I waited for him to pay the man before I approached him. I stepped forward and asked the friar, "Excuse me father, can you tell me at what point, do the locals cross the river?"

Before he could answer, his nanny goat spun around and accidentally knocked me over. I fell to the ground landing on my injured arm and cried out in pain.

The friar helped me up and said, "I am ever so sorry lad."

After the pain eased I told him, "It's alright, it wasn't your fault it was an accident."

He looked at my bound up arm and said, "Oh my poor lad, what have you done to yourself?"

I answered, "A wolf attacked me last night. My companion bound it up for me."

The kind friar said, "Dear, dear lad, you need to have your arm seen to quickly before it turns bad. You and your companion must come with me to our Abbey across the other side of the river. There is no ford to cross but I have a boat that is big enough for the three of us, and the goat."

I explained to him, "I also have a horse."

He chuckled and said, "He is very welcome to swim behind."

After I told Tianaju about the friar's kind offer, all five of us went down to the river. The friar tied Lianga to the boat, and off we went. The river was wide and calm, and the friar was big and strong, so it didn't take him long to row over to the other side. We walked for about an hour before eventually reaching the abbey.

The friar gave the goat to one of his waiting brothers then turned to me and said, "Brother James will tend to your lovely horse. Now, come with me the both of you, we must dress your wounds before they go bad. By the way my name is Brother Martin."

He took us into his medicine room and made up a creamy compound of herbs. After bathing my arm, he spread the compound onto the wounds, and bound it with a long clean white cloth. He then gave me a spoonful of medicine, and told me to keep the bottle and take a spoonful three times a day. Tianaju and I thanked him for doing such a wonderful job.

He replied, "Well, it's the least I can do after the nanny goat knocked you over. All we can offer you now is supper and two rooms for the night. Before retiring to bed you are welcome to join us in our evening prayers. So if you will follow me I'll take you to your rooms."

The rooms were small and the skinny bed was hard but a lot softer than the floor. Before Brother Martin left us he told us that we were welcome to wander around the Abbey and its grounds.

It was a sunny day so it was very enjoyable walking around the lovely Abbey and sitting on a bench in the flower garden. My arm felt a little easier now so I fell asleep and only woke when I heard the gong sounding for supper. When I opened my eyes I saw that my head was lying on Tianaju's lap, and that I was looking up at her lovely eyes. She told me that I had been sleeping for hours. I got up and thanked her for nursing me while I slept. She told me that it was quite alright because she had slept as well. So supper, evening prayers and bed finished the day perfectly.

In the morning my arm felt much better. I could open and close my fingers a small bit now. So Brother Martin had done an excellent job. We both joined the brothers for morning prayers, then a bowl of porridge for breakfast. Later that morning I asked Brother Martin if he knew the route to Thurso.

He informed me, "Firstly you will have to cross the wide Beauly Firth lad. I know the fishermen there, so I will ask them to take you over. From then on you just follow the coast and you'll find it. But you are to stay here for at least three to four days before you go anywhere with that arm laddie. It needs to be treated twice daily."

So you could say that the next four days were a blessing, so to speak, because it was so peaceful.

My arm was feeling a lot better after the rest and the swelling had gone down considerably. Brother Martin took a look at it and gave me the go ahead for early the following morning.

The next day we were up early—the same time as a glorious sunrise. Brother James brought a brown donkey and Lianga out from their stables to join us out in the yard. The brown donkey was for

Brother Martin. We thanked all the brothers, mounted our rides and walked away heading for the Firth.

It took us about two hours to reach it, and to our amazement it was extremely wide. The fishermen told the friar that they were happy to take us over, free of charge. We thanked Brother Martin and told him that he would never be forgotten as we waved good bye.

It was a large sailing boat with oars so Lianga didn't have to swim behind. As we rowed away across the wide Beauly Firth, Tianaju kept herself well covered up the whole time."

Half way across the firth we heard the fishermen talking among themselves. "Have you noticed the moon isn't as bright these last two months?" asked, Captain Conor.

"Yes, we have, do you know the reason why captain? Is there an eclipse going on"?

"No!" replied Captain Conor. "According to the sailors it is happening all over the world. They say that down around the south end of the world the moon is getting even dimmer. All the seas are shrinking back, leaving miles and miles of sandy rocky beaches. It's happening up this way too."

"Gosh!" they all shouted. "Why, are they shrinking captain?"

"They are shrinking because there is very little tide now to bring them back. The seas are unusually calm with very little waves."

The concerned captain then shook his head and continued, "Some say the end of the world is coming and that we will all shrivel up and die."

They all looked at one another in disbelief.

The captain encouraged them by saying, "Don't worry lads, it hasn't happened yet. Come on! Let's get our passengers over safely before the river dries up."

They all laughed and said, "Aye, aye captain."

When we reached the other side, and after thanking the captain and his crew, all three of us walked off along the coast for a while until my stomach recovered from that rock and rolling ride.

Tianaju looked worried and said to me, "Let's hope we get to Howler in time Welusa. It looks as if Ohibronoeler is slowly winning."

"Don't worry," I told her. "He is not far away now. Brother Martin told me Thurso is only two days from here."

I then asked, "When we get there will we be able to see Howler from the shore?"

She replied, "Yes, he is big enough to be seen for miles."

As soon as my stomach felt better we mounted Lianga and headed on along the coastal road.

It was once again a nice sunny day but the sea breeze was cutting into our faces, so we put up our hoods to protect them. I could open and close my hand better now. My fingers were almost back to normal but my arm was still very tender to touch.

As night was beginning to draw in, we stopped outside some woods, not far from a castle. I found out later, from a passerby, that it was called Dunrobin Castle. As we were lying down resting beside our camp fire, we saw the dragon sailing across the dim half-moon. He was a lot darker now and I could see his amber eyes more clearly. He caught site of us lying there and swooped down and hovered above us laughing.

"Ha, you pair of fools. I am just biding my time waiting for you to waste yours. Oh, what a shame pretty one. You should have married me when you had the chance. I'll never marry you now, however much you beg me to. You were rotten to me and I will never forgive you. You are nothing but a sneaky flirt and a dreadful liar. Get rid of her, Welusa, before she leaves you with a broken heart the same way she broke mine. Oh! My poor boy, what has she done to your arm? Have you been biting again, Tianaju? She used to bite me every night, Welusa, just to make me cry then laughed at me as I wept and wept begging her to stop."

He coiled himself up into a snake like form and slithered across the ground towards us. He led there staring at me with half closed amber eyes studying my shirt pocket. I put my hand on my pocket just in case he made a grab for the lock of hair.

He just laughed and said, "Pah, that doesn't worry me, Welusa. Since the last time we met, my power has tripled. I don't need any more moonbeams now. But! I will still swallow the rest of them anyway."

He then slithered away, uncoiling himself back into the dragon, and slowly sailed up towards the moon saying, "Bring on the winds. They are all going to die. All of you are going to die."

"Well" I said, "That was a mouthful. I couldn't even get a word in. Come on Tianaju let's get some sleep."

We laid out our blankets, led down and went to sleep listening to the night birds and a solitary vixen crying in the distance.

The sunrise the following morning was spectacular. It made the woodland glow like rippling flames flickering through the wavering trees. This made us feel happy as we started out once again around the coast.

I said to Tianaju, "We should be in Thurso by tomorrow afternoon. I hope it stays fine for us until then, otherwise we may not be able to see Howler out at sea."

She replied confidently, "Oh, you will see him alright, but even if you can't, you will hear him and he will hear you."

I told Lianga that my arm was feeling a lot better now and asked him if he would canter instead of walking. He replied, "Okay Welusa, the quicker we finish this the better."

So away we went stopping every now and then for a rest, some bread and a few boiled eggs that the brothers gave us and some milk. Riding Lianga was very tiring and sometimes painful, so a rest was much appreciated by us all.

Just like the spectacular sunrise, there was an equally beautiful sunset. As the last ray disappeared over the horizon we came across a large rock rising out from the earth. It was about twelve or thirteen feet tall and three or four feet wide and almost as thick. There were people camped in a field opposite, so I asked them if they knew anything about it.

They replied, "It's always been here, there are more of them in this area too."

I asked, "What is the name of this place?"

One lady answered, "It's called the Land of Stones. We don't know where they came from, in fact no one knows. But some say that the stones are haunted. So be careful."

I thanked them and wished them good night. I pitched up our tent while Tianaju sat besides the stone looking up in wonder. I didn't mention anything about the stones being haunted. After I had finished setting up the old but waterproof tent I joined her and jokingly asked, "Well, shall we have bread and cheese or shall we have cheese and bread?"

She answered, "Well, I think we'll have no bread and cheese, and definitely no cheese or bread either, not even eggs."

I asked her, "Why not?"

She replied, "Because there's none left. The camper's dog just scoffed the lot along with my last apple."

I said, "What! Where is he? Wait until I catch the greedy twerp. I'll give him what for."

She burst out laughing and said, "I am only kidding, but it was funny seeing your face."

I said, "Oh you, I'll get you for that."

We had our supper and bedded down for the night, looking forward to meeting Howler hopefully the following afternoon. As we slept we were awakened by someone groaning with a deep man's voice. We listened and he groaned again saying, "Who are you? Get away from here, you dare sleep before me. This is my place; it belongs to me and my friends. We are also friends with the dragon. Go away now, we don't like you Welusa or I will crush you where you lie."

"It's the stone! He's talking to us. We had better move Welusa or he will crush us," said Tianaju anxiously.

I thought to myself, "How can stones talk." I could see that she was worried about me, so I said, "Okay, come on, it's really dark out there but we'll pack up and go somewhere else."

As soon as I climbed out of the tent I heard a roar of laughter. It was Ohibronoeler, the dragon. He was pretending to be the stone talking.

"Ha, ha, ha. Boo, what a pair of scaredy-cats. Fancy you being afraid, of a little old stone. Well, well. Tut, tut, what little babies you are. Ho ho ho. I'm off I can't stick it any longer. Goodbye baby Welusa."

I shouted back, as he zoomed off, "Yeah, and a good riddance too."

I climbed back in and said, "Come on let's get back to sleep, it's only the nutty dragon."

Later during the night it began to rain but fortunately just before dawn it stopped. I was excited now but a little nervous as we ventured out on our last lap. We were not following the coast anymore. Instead the road was now heading towards mountains. It was well into the afternoon before I noticed that we were being watched and followed by what looked like a band of Highlanders. As we were passing through the valley, I could hear whistling every now and then. It was like as if these people were communicating with one another. I told Tianaju to disappear then asked Lianga to go a little faster.

He said, "Yes I will. I have seen them Welusa, they have been following us for some time now."

So we raced on to get clear of the mountains and out into the open. I couldn't feel the queen behind me any more so I knew she was gone. We were almost out and into the clear when a gang of rough looking highlanders jumped up in front of us coming from both sides. They were pulling a large net between them. Lianga stopped and because I was only holding on with one hand I slipped off. I ordered him to run away and not to worry about me. He turned and galloped off up the side of the mountain and out of sight. The highlanders grabbed me and tied my hands behind my back. I cried out with pain as they twisted my damaged arm. They put me onto a horse drawn cart that they had hidden in some bushes. I was then taken to their camp and put into a cage made of wood, tied together with ropes.

I asked them, "Why are you keeping me captive? What have I done?"

But no one could understand me, and neither could I understand them. They would not come too close to me either. It looked very much as if they were afraid of me. I was just about to ask them again when someone shouted, "QUIET."

It was the head of the gang walking towards me asking questions. I could hardly make out what he was saying, as he was speaking in a type of Scottish slang English language. If I was to write down exactly how he spoke to me you would never understand it either.

He stood his distance and shouted out the same thing over and over until I eventually worked out what he was saying, "You are a sorcerer. What are you doing with that dragon? Where has your witch gone?"

I shouted back, "I am not a sorcerer and neither do I have any witch with me. I am just traveling to Thurso to see someone."

He stared at me and said, "Yes, another sorcerer. I know him well and he will be the next one to die. My men have been watching you and your misty hairy dragon, creeping around Scotland. WHERE, is he? Tell me now!"

I answered him saying, "I haven't got a dragon. I don't know how you think that I have one."

He shouted out, "LIAR! Take him away lads and leave him to starve."

Eight men picked up my cage and took me to the top of a mountain. They hoisted me up in the cage over a branch of a large tree then ran away, leaving me dangling about twenty feet off the ground.

It wasn't long before my pocket started tingling and I got a poke in the back. It was Tianaju, sitting right behind me.

I assured her saying, "I am okay. Don't worry, as soon as I can untie myself, I'll get out and we'll be away from here."

She said, "I know you will think of something, I have great faith in you."

I joked with her saying, "I will be glad when this mission is over, because I could do with a bit of magic for a change. It would make life a lot easier."

I struggled for about an hour before I finally got my good hand free. I sat down to get my breath back and to think how to get out of the cage. I got up and looked all around it and to my surprise I found that it would be easy. The men were so afraid of me that they only tied two simple knots in the gate. So I undid them easy enough. I opened the gate and because of my injured arm it was a painful struggle climbing onto the roof and monkey climbing the thin rope. It took me awhile but I eventually managed to clamber onto and across the branch and down the tree. I fell the last three feet to the ground and hurt my arm again. So I waited until the pain went away before I said, "Come on let's get from here before they come back. Where's Lianga?"

"He is behind you," she replied.

I turned and said, "Oh yeah, come on lets go before they come back."

Off we went and there was no way they were going to catch us this time. We were away and probably out of sight before they knew we were gone

When we were far enough away, we stopped and rested. My injured arm was aching now from struggling with those ropes. I led down exhausted and drifted off to sleep until Tianaju woke me up saying, "Listen."

I listened a while and said, "It's him, it's Howler!"

I got to my feet and realised that we were now on the coast near Thurso. As I looked out to the sea I could see that he was facing north. He was gigantic and looked like a massive swarm of black bees sweeping across the cold North Sea. But as he drew in the icy cold air from an ocean full of icebergs, he turned pure white. Then with a lovely howling sound he blew this freezing cold air up to his father in the North Pole and then turned black again.

I said, "Well this is it. Let's go and get him."

We trotted off to get closer to the coast, so that he could see me waving. I found a perfect spot on a hill close to the cliffs. Alongside us was a large tower. So I stood there waiting until he howled up another blast of cold air to his father. Suddenly, I noticed that the moment he stopped howling it looked as if he was falling dropping out of the sky towards the sea. He then quickly recovered and began to sweep again.

I immediately asked, "Did you see that?"

"I did. He must be weakening Welusa," replied Tianaju.

I quickly shouted, "Howler, Howler, I'm over here, over here." He stopped and spun around.

I began to wave and shout again to let him know where I was, "I'm over here."

He slowly moved towards the cliffs and stared at me. He had a strange look in his eyes then roared, "Are you another sorcerer? If you are, I'll blow you to kingdom come. Speak! Tell me who you are?"

My throat was dry now so I could hardly talk. He roared again, "SPEAK!"

I took a deep breath, swallowed and said, "My name is Welusa. I have an important message for you. It's from the Emerald Queen of children, she is here beside me."

He roared back, "No one can speak to me unless they have magic powers. So you are either telling me the truth or you are a sorcerer. If the queen is with you, prove it to me?"

I answered, "I don't know how I can. All I have is a lock of her hair."

He roared again, "Pah! Rubbish, that's rubbish; any one can have a lock of hair."

I thought and said, "If I was a sorcerer I would be afraid of you and your power. Wouldn't I?"

He snapped back, "Don't try to be clever sonny, no one can trick me."

He drew in his breath, picked me up and dropped me into the cold North Sea. As I splashed about trying to catch my breath, he looked at me with his scowling eyes, and said, "Now I will see if you are telling me the truth."

He picked me out of the cold sea and placed me back on the hill again saying, "Hmm, if you were a sorcerer you wouldn't be wet. So show me the lock of her hair?"

I was so cold that it took me a while to take the leather pouch out of my pocket. I was shivering as I showed it to him saying, "Here it is. It's ... it's as dry as a b-bone. It never gets wet. Take a look?"

His angry face changed to a friendlier one now as he assured me, "No, no, no. I believe you now. I was just testing you, that's all. What does the queen want? Tell me her message?"

I gave him exactly the same message as I gave the others. I told him of my plan to frost up the dragon but didn't know how I could toss the lock of hair. I also mentioned to him that the dragon would be in mid Scotland during the next full moon.

He moved from side to side thinking for a while. So I asked him, "Have you been feeling weak lately?"

He answered, "Yes. So that's why I have been tiring every now and then. It was the dragon sapping my energy. So he is the reason the seas are shrinking away from the shores eh."

He came up to me, looked me in my eyes and said, "Why didn't you tell me that in the first place, sonny."

Before I could say, "I tried to tell you," he took off swirling in the air and howled, "Tell her I'm on my way. I will be back tomorrow afternoon. So wait for me Welusa. Don't worry I the great Howler, will lift you up to toss the lock of hair."

I watched him as he howled his way, weaving in and out those cold icebergs, over the fabulous, but treacherous looking North Sea.

Tianaju gave me a big hug and once again thanked me.

I sat down and said, "I am really glad it's all over now."

She replied, "It isn't over yet Welusa. There is worse to come."

I sat down and agreed saying, "Yes, I know. What I really meant was, I am glad that I have given all the sons your message. But now I suppose we have to go back to the middle of Scotland?"

She replied, "Let us wait and hear what Howler has to say first."

I was soaking wet and cold now so I set up camp and changed. I then gathered some wood and lit a fire to warm me up and dry my wet clothes

Tianaju and I had our last pieces of bread and cheese. Lianga went wandering off to graze, while we sat and watched the shrinking ocean struggling to get back to shore.

When night came we climbed into our tent and led down. She took her glowing wand from the sash around her waist to give us some light. She was quiet for a while then asked, "If we have to go back to the middle of Scotland can we go to Dunkeld?"

"Yes, why not," I replied. "We had some fun there didn't we?"

"Yes we did Welusa. It would be nice to walk through the woods again. It is such a lovely place."

"Yes it is, I loved it there too, Tianaju."

She paused again then said, "If your mission is successful and we have defeated Ohibronoeler, I would like to repay all the kind folk that gave us help and shelter. Will you come with me?"

I thought for a while then said, "Well I might."

She sat up asking, "Are you teasing me again Welusa?"

I laughed as I gave her a poke for a change and replied, "Of course I will. I would love to."

She gave a big sigh, squeezed my hand and said, "Thank you." Then turned over tucking her wand back into her sash.

I lay there feeling so happy that I began to wonder to myself again, "Is this real? Is this really happening to me? How can I talk to the winds, birds and animals? Is there really a dragon? I have been traveling with someone more beautiful than any human has ever seen. What if this is just a dream and I'm going to wake up finding she's gone. Wow I hope it isn't."

I turned over still thinking away until I fell asleep.

The next thing I knew, Tianaju was nudging me saying, "Come on sleepy head time to get up, we have no breakfast so we had better go and get some."

I asked, "Where from?"

"From the beach," she replied.

We went down to the beach and she collected a small bag of sea weed, and said, "That will do nicely."

I looked at it saying, "Well it certainly doesn't look like it."

She informed me, "It will be nice when it's cooked."

We went back to the camp and lit a fire. She asked me to take the pan and fetch some water from the stream. So I did, and after she cooked the sloppy looking stuff, she called me to come and sit down. I sat down to face a full bowl of what looked like an old squashed black cabbage.

She said, "Go on try it. You will enjoy it. It's lovely."

So to give you an idea of what it was like, it took me three goes to get it to stay on the spoon. Every time I picked it up it slid straight off the side and on to my lap. Eventually I mastered it and began to, half-heartedly, nibble a piece, or should I say lick a piece. To my surprise it didn't taste too bad, it tasted worse! So as not to offend her, I reluctantly forced it down me. It took me an hour to finish it and by that time it was cold. I was now feeling like a sheep chewing its cud.

She then said to me, "There now, wasn't that lovely?"

I replied with a burp as I finished my last slop, "Yes I really enjoyed it."

She smiled and asked, "Would you like some more?"

I answered, "No its okay you can finish it."

She replied, "That will do for now, we'll save some for lunch."

I remember saying to myself, with tears my eyes, "Sea weed for lunch. I must be dreaming?"

In the afternoon after our lovely, lovely lunch, we sat down by the tent waiting for the return of Howler.

Lianga who was grazing beside us looked at me and said, "You look very messy Welusa. Have you been eating grass?"

I shook my head and replied, "No just seaweed."

I was sure I heard him laugh as he turned around and walked away.

Tianaju was the first to see Howler and shouted, "Look! There he is," and pointed towards an Island way in the distance. I looked and saw a swirling black mass above an Island out in the cold sea heading towards us.

He was really howling this time as if he was in a hurry. As he approached the coast he calmed down, and stayed hovering above the shore.

"Welusa!" He hollered. "I have news from my father. He believes in your message and is on his way to his brothers. He hadn't noticed the dragon because he was too busy cooling down the world this summer. The only thing he did notice was that his power was getting weaker. He wants to know where you intend to attack him, so that they can work out a plan."

I shouted back, "I am so pleased that he believed me. Can you tell him that we should attack the dragon above Dunkeld. It's as good a place as any."

"That sounds good to me. I will tell my father." He then asked, "In the meantime, how are you going to get there before the next full moon?"

I told him that Lianga is a powerful horse and that he will get us there on time.

"Where is the queen?" he asked.

I replied, "She is behind me."

He swayed to and fro as if he was thinking again, and said, "Pack up your tent and belongings and be on your way."

He stayed there watching us as he slowly paced the shore. After we had packed and mounted.

I waved and said, "Thank you, Howler. We'll see you in Dunkeld."

Then as we turned to ride away, Howler shouted, "Hah! You must be joking. You will never get to Dunkeld in time."

After saying that, he gave out a loud howl and rushed towards me, and roared, "POWER! You say your horse has POWER, sonny. Well I'll show you power, lad."

Then in just one swift movement he swept all three of us into the air heading south.

He laughed and said, "This is power boy, REAL POWER. Keep your face covered and your mouth closed Welusa; there are a lot of flies about."

Howler was right because if I hadn't have covered my face, I would have been battered by millions of them. It must have taken us at least two hours before he gently set us down alongside the river in Dunkeld.

"How is that Welusa my dear friend?"

I replied "Fantastic! I wonder what your father's like?"

"Ho, ho, you'll know it, when you see and hear him, lad. I have to go now but I will be back to let you know my father's plan. So I'll see you soon kid. Bye for now."

We watched and listened to him howl out of sight then I sat down and said, "That was great but it was cold up there."

So while Tianaju was busy brushing flies off of poor Lianga, I set up camp and made a fire to warm us up. I was now looking forward to three days of rest before the full moon, but I didn't know what we were going to do for food.

Later on, after I had recovered from the unexpected ride through the air, Tianaju surprised me by saying, "Come on, pack up camp, we are off to find an Inn. We need some food, a bath, and a bed for the night."

I asked her, "I thought you said you were not allowed to help me."

She answered, "I'm not. You have shared your money with me. Now I am sharing mine with you. If it wasn't for me, you would have more than enough money left."

"Oh, in that case, I'll have three suppers, and a nice soft bed," I joked.

She replied, "I don't think so. A soft bed maybe, but the rest, no, no, no."

I just laughed and began packing up.

Dunkeld is a nice quiet little village with two stores, two Inns and a tavern. One of the Inns also had a stable. I went inside the Inn and to my surprise the inn keeper was a lady. This made it easier for the queen to walk in without completely covering her face.

I booked a stable, and two rooms then asked, "Could we have two baths please?"

She replied, "Yes, but we only have one bath tub."

I replied, "That's okay I'll go first."

Tianaju scowled at me. I looked at the landlady and laughed. She knew I was only kidding.

I then asked her, "Later, could we have whatever is on the menu for supper please?"

"Certainly," she replied. "My daughter will now show you to your rooms, and will call you when the bath is ready."

My room was cosy with a nice bed. It wasn't soft, but I didn't care. I lay there until it was my turn for a bath. When my turn finally came, I enjoyed it and felt clean and fresh once again. My arm was now healing up nicely so I didn't bother to bandage it.

When the gong rang for supper I met her highness outside her room. Once again she looked amazing in a green dress with long sleeves and matching shoes. She had a black scarf over her head that matched the sash around her waist.

She tapped her sash, smiled, and said, "Don't look so worried. I have my wand with me, don't I?"

I smiled back and said, "Yes, I forgot about that."

Although we were constantly being watched, our supper of bacon, cabbage and potatoes went down nicely with a cup of warm milk for bed. We decided to have an early night as we were looking forward to sleeping in a real bed for a change. I said good night to my beautiful companion, walked into my room and collapsed on top of the bed. I fell sound asleep until I got a poke in the back again.

I knew it was Tianaju so I turned around and said, "Oh no it's you again."

She smiled and said, "There's a nice mattress on the floor."

I said, "What!"

She told me again, "There's a nice mattress on the floor for you."

"You have your own room and a nice bed," I told her.

"I know," she said. "But it's too lonely in there for me. That is why I've brought my nice mattress in for you."

I groaned and said, "Well, it's no use asking how you got in, because you probably came through the keyhole and the mattress. Oh well, I guess I'm back on the floor then."

I rolled over, fell on the mattress, said good night and went to sleep saying to myself, "I thought it was too good to be true. I hope I snore all night."

The following morning I woke up and found myself lying on the hard floor. Tianaju was back in her own room and so was her mattress.

For breakfast we had a nice bowl of porridge, and then went shopping for food supplies. Later we collected Lianga and went down to the river. Lianga wanted to know if we had bought some carrots for him. I told him that we had and gave him a few. The weather was dull and drizzly, so we sat on a bench underneath the bridge until the sun came out before we went for a walk.

"Don't worry about me I'll stay here and munch some of this nice fresh grass," said Lianga.

So we strolled along and found a trail that led us up a twisted path to the top of a steep hill. There were tall rocky cliffs on the one side looking out at a lovely view. When we got to the top, the view was even lovelier. We could see all of the valley below and the river racing away through it.

We sat there admiring it all, until suddenly we heard a woman's voice ranting and raving. It was coming from behind a large rock. We made our way towards the rock, behind which, we found a thin ragged woman. I could tell by the charms hanging around her neck that she was a Soothsayer. She sat there with a pipe in her mouth rolling out some tobacco. She grabbed my arm with her long bony fingers and pulled me close. The smell of tobacco on her breath made me cough as she warned me, "My name is Nan. Beware! I have foreseen a great catastrophe here in Scotland. Behold the moon, its light is fading. Soon it will be darkened by an unstoppable powerful force."

She stopped for a while, before asking, "Have you got a flint to light my pipe, laddie?"

I coughed a few more times before replying, "I am sorry, I haven't brought any with me."

She slumped back and said, "Oh well, be on your way then, but take heed of my warning."

As we walked back down, the bell rang out in the Cathedral bell tower.

"Shall we stay at the Inn again tonight Welusa? It will be the last night before the full moon, so you will need a good night's rest."

I replied, "Yes, that's fine by me. I'm sure Lianga will enjoy another night in a nice snug stable."

We headed back to where he was waiting for us and passed on the good news to him. I told him that he would be enjoying another night of luxury. This made him jump for joy as we headed off back to the Inn.

The Landlady was happy to see us and asked, "Is it the same rooms tonight Welusa?"

"Yes please and supper too," I replied.

I told her that we had already put Lianga in the stables. She said that was fine and gave me the keys to our rooms.

Later that night Tianaju came into my room and told me, "I have just been talking to Angela the lovely owl. She informed me that the dragon is black and enormous now."

"Don't worry," I assured her. "We have the mighty winds on our side. I am not worried about the dragon, because I have something in my pocket that he doesn't like. Come on, let's go and have our supper so that we can have an early night."

We had our supper and went to bed feeling a lot better for having it. Once again I just led down on top of the bed saying to myself, "I am not bothering to get in, because I expect she'll be in now shortly."

I lay there waiting and must have fallen asleep because when I woke up in the morning I was still on my bed. I stretched out and lay there for a while. As I slowly turned over to get off the bed, to my surprise the beautiful queen was lying there on the floor. She was covered up on her mattress and fast asleep. I poked her and said, "Hey come on sleepy fairy, wake up. What are you doing down there?"

She yawned, and answered, "I don't like being lonely and you needed your rest."

I laughed and said, "You should have told me, I wouldn't have minded."

She looked at me and smiled, took out her glowing wand and with a puff of magic she vanished, and so did her mattress.

We had some toast for breakfast and then set off down to the river and sat on the bank watching the fish coming up for flies. Later, we went walking through the lovely woods again. On our way back we played the same game of throwing sticks in the water. That was great fun again and once more she won six sticks to four. Mid-afternoon we went for a walk up to the Cathedral. The structure of the building itself, together with the internal scheme, was a work of art. In fact, one could say that the whole cathedral must have been designed by a genius.

While sitting outside on the wall waiting for Howler I was beginning to feel very nervous. I wasn't nervous because I was afraid. I was just worrying about what would happen if things went wrong.

It was early evening before Howler finally arrived hovering above the tall larch trees.

He explained the plan of action to me saying, "As Ohibronoeler comes in tonight swallowing up more of the moonbeams, my cousins and I will patrol the ground level to prevent the dragon diving for cover among the trees. My father and my uncle, the South Wind, will come in blowing towards each other. My other uncles the East and West will also blow towards one another. Hopefully they will trap him long enough to frost him up. When they have achieved this, I will take you up to the dragon to toss in the lock of Tianaju's hair. If for any reason they cannot trap him, don't worry they have a few back up plans in mind."

"That sounds good to me," I said.

He suggested, "Try and get some rest Welusa, to prepare yourself for an awesome battle."

He then twisted up and away shouting, "See you later kid."

That evening I couldn't rest. All I did was pace up and down the river bank talking to myself until dark. During this time I tripped over about three or four mole hills and fell head first into one. So if I was to prepare for battle my face was certainly ready for it.

It seemed a very long night, as we watched and waited for some sign of the dragon. It wasn't until way after midnight that we saw him. He had grown to twice his size and there were streaks of lightning, flickering and flashing all through him.

The moon was dim but the dragon's flashes lit up the sky as he sailed over us. He was as black as a thunder cloud before a storm, and was every bit as frightening. As we watched him swallowing up more of the moonbeams we could hear a roar in the distance. It was the winds. They had been waiting for him and were now on their way in.

Ohibronoeler stopped and scanned the sky and shouted, "Come on you bag of winds I'm ready for you!"

He circled around, stopped and waited. The winds were getting closer and louder now. There were animals running everywhere, frantically looking for cover. The massive North, East, South and West Winds were at least four times the size of their sons and were closing in on him at his level. Their sons were coming in at tree top level.

The dragon just stayed there laughing, calling them a bunch of old wind bags and beckoning them saying, "Come on! I'll teach you a lesson you'll never forget. But there again you won't be around to remember it, will you, ha, ha."

I heard Soaker call to me, "Get under the bridge Welusa."

All three of us went under the bridge and watched as the winds closed in. The tremendous roar and howl of them must have been terrifying for the villagers.

They couldn't hear the dragon but I could hear him as he roared out, "I see you brought your babies with you. Well say hello to one of mine."

After saying that, he opened up his mouth and blasted out a clap of thunder, hitting Soaker square in the middle. This sent him hurtling down into the trees, breaking some of them in half. The dragon quickly sent out three more that sent the other sons crashing into the nearby trees, hay barns and mountains.

"Ah, poor little babies. Go and wipe their noses, daddies."

The four sons recovered and went back to their posts and began to blow towards one another. The father winds did the same and zoomed in on the dragon, but he was ready for them. He curled up into a black ball and fired out sheets of lightning from every part of himself. At the same time there were numerous mighty claps of thunder, stunning the winds, scattering them across the mountains and up and down the valley. They slowly regrouped while the sons were once again sent crashing to the ground with more vicious cracks of thunder. The great winds attacked the dragon three more times but each time they suffered the same fate.

Once again the dragon blasted out another round of thunder and lightning sending the disorientated sons tumbling back again. The lightning flashed into an oak tree and another one hit a barn setting both of them alight. If it wasn't for Soaker putting them out with his wet breath, the forest would have caught alight and the barn would have burnt down. The four sons slowly regained their posts as their fathers moved in to attack.

Ohibronoeler uncurled himself back into his full dragon form and rushed at the West Wind shooting out another streak of lightning followed by a crack of thunder. This once again knocked him back stunning him badly. While he was in this stunned state the dragon tried to slip past him. The South Wind quickly closed the gap and blew the dragon back. The dragon retaliated and blasted the South Wind back hurtling into his brother. He then spun around as the East and North wind came in to attack. They both blew together squeezing him in-between them, only to be sent spinning backwards in shock from a huge deafening clap of thunder. The winds repositioned themselves and stayed a safe distance away.

Ohibronoeler curled and twisted himself around and around constantly watching for their next move. He was snarling and spitting out little menacing flashes of lightning saying, "Come on you bunch of miserable old wind bags. I'll pop you every time. If you want to die I'll be kind to you. I'll let you die in my arms, and bury you at sea. How is that for compassion? Oh boys, boys, don't be fools. I love you all. Don't listen to Welusa he's a Sorcerer. He is the thief that is stealing the moonbeams I am trying to put them back. So what do you say? Do you want to listen to him and die, or will you listen to me and live?"

The North Wind spread himself and roared, "Do you think we are fools? We are just having fun playing with you. It's you that is going to die not us. Oh, and by the way, we will not be burying you at sea either. It will be in the garbage dump. So what do you think of that Ohibronoeler?"

The dragon was furious now and once again began to shoot out a barrage of thunder and lightning from all around him. He rushed at the North Wind who immediately retreated away. As he did so, the South Wind closed in from behind and the East and West came in from the sides. The dragon turned and knocked them back with more vicious claps of thunder. As he did this, the North Wind advanced and drew in his breath drawing the dragon back away from his brothers. This ferocious battle went on relentlessly, until the winds calmed down.

By this time the whole village was awake. They had all been franticly tying things down in fear of them blowing away. I could now hear mothers shouting to their children, "Stay inside don't come out, get under the bed." Others were shouting, "Get under the table."

There were people screaming as they tried to get to the Cathedral for protection. It was one of the safest buildings there was to shelter in.

The winds were doing their best trying to keep the dragon away from the village but could not protect the village from themselves. Their ferocious battle with him created a hurricane that ripped through the village, tearing the roofs off thatched cottages and tiles from other houses. There were carts and barrels flying through the air crashing down, smashing into smithereens as they hit the streets and buildings. Even a small tree was ripped up and crashed on top of the bridge we were hiding under. If it wasn't for the sons keeping the dragon up in the air he would have wiped out the whole village with fire.

The great winds after a little rest began to roar again. The dragon looked extremely stressed now but still managed to say, "What's, the matter girls? Had enough? Why don't you go and powder your noses. Oh, how I weep for you. Oh girls, girls, don't be foolish. Think of the poor people below and how you have destroyed their lovely homes."

The North Wind just laughed and said, "Take a look at yourself dopey?"

The dragon replied, "Why should I? I am not vain like you bunch of ladies. In fact I hate my power. I hate it so much I'm going to give you some more of it."

He curled himself up into a ball again and bolted out another blaze of lightening, followed by more heavy claps of thunder. Once again this blasted the great winds, scattering them uncontrollably backwards. The sons kept the dragon from escaping while the great winds recovered. So Ohibronoeler dived down and smashed them too, with seething bolts of lightning, followed by savage thunder balls exploding right in front of them. This sent them once again ripping through the well broken up forest, trees and fences across the land.

The great winds by now had reorganised themselves and were once again homing in on the dragon.

The North Wind called out to him saying, "Why don't you take a look at yourself, snowy?"

Ohibronoeler uncurled and slyly looked at himself. He was surprised to see that he was beginning to turn grey.

The North Wind was quick to tell him, "Yes! That's right; Mister Menace your nasty energy is being drained now. So what do you think of that BOY?"

"Rubbish!" shouted the dragon as he fired out another round of thunder. They were far enough away not to be knocked back but it stunned them momentarily. They slowly moved back in again taunting him, teasing him the whole time. The dragon just laughed, curled up and sent them screaming back with a ferocious blast of thunder. He then bolted out streaks of lightning in the shape of arms and legs. As soon as they hit the ground it was like as if they were running towards the Cathedral. One of them smashed into the Cathedral bell tower splitting it in half, causing it to come crashing down through the roof. The other two flashed into the village hall and store setting them both alight. The raging dragon bolted out two more that smashed into the Cathedral door and porch, completely destroying them. He was laughing all the time this was happening. But his laughter soon turned to anguish as the four winds caught him unexpectedly. They came in blowing from all sides and squeezed him in the middle. This made him release more savage streaks of lightning followed by a huge explosion of thunder that sent them all tumbling back once more.

He uncurled himself and shouted, "Who said my energy is being drained? Do you want to see some more, or do you give up. Hey Mister Northy where are you? O yeah, I see you now, sniveling over there, stuck in the mountain. Come to me child and I'll dry your eyes for you, ha ha ha."

I could see the dragon was getting paler now with every action that he made. Then suddenly, he caught sight of me looking out from underneath the bridge. He stretched out his arm with the small red claw and shouted, "Yes, Welusa! You will pay for this."

He opened his mouth and bolted out a streak of lightning at me. It missed, but split a tree beside the bridge sending it crashing across the river. By this time the winds had recovered and were circling the dragon taunting him saying, "Hey snowy, take a look at yourself, loser. Come on! Is that the best you can do? We are enjoying ourselves playing around with you."

Ohibronoeler was looking worried now. He knew his energy was being drained so he began looking for an escape route. Every time he tried, he was blown back into the middle again. The winds backed off and circled him once more. The dragon was more grey than black now, except for the middle. I could see the centre of him was now red as fire.

The North wind gave a signal to stop circling and immediately there was silence. My ears were ringing from the tremendous deafening noise of the battle. So I covered them for a while until my hearing came back. The winds looked as if they were talking to one another, but I couldn't hear a thing. They went silent again and so did the dragon. It looked as if they were listening to something. It was not long before I could hear what it was they were listening to. It was a roar in the distance coming from all around us. As it got louder and louder I could see there were more winds coming our way. The roar was almost deafening again as the four strange winds reached us. Each one stopped in between the North, East, South, and West Winds. To my surprise I heard Toaster shout, "Oh no! Our Mothers are here."

One of the mothers answered, "We weren't going to let you have the entire fun boys."

I turned to Tianaju and shouted, "You didn't tell me they had mothers."

She shouted back, "I forgot to tell you. They are the North East, North West, South East, and South West Winds."

The dragon was now completely surrounded. The only place left for him to go was up. So he coiled himself like a spring and torpedoed up into the air. It was no use because the winds just followed him making him dive back down again. He was then stopped in his tracks by the sons.

This went on for a while as the dragon tried to escape, until he stopped in the middle and started laughing, and shouted, "Yahoo, now that's what I call fun. Did you enjoy that, girls? Well, well, well fancy bringing the mammies with you. Dear, dear, dear, you should all be ashamed of your selves. Well, if I am going down by a bunch of girls, at least I will be going down a man. So come on! I've been saving the best until last."

As the winds closed in on him he took a deep breath and rushed towards the three North Winds blowing out flames of fire, followed by tremendous claps of thunder. Boom, boom! This sent them tumbling uncontrollable backwards again. The dragon then headed for the gap but was stopped by the South and East winds. He retreated and took in another breath and rushed towards them bellowing out massive fire balls that exploded viciously in front of them. This also sent them tumbling backwards across the valley leaving a big gap. By this time the North winds had fully recovered and blocked his escape. The dragon now turned his attention to the West wind and charged him blasting out ferocious flames of fire. Fortunately for the West Wind, and disappointingly for the dragon, the West Wind was used to the heat and just laughed at him. The dragon retreated back into the middle and stayed there hovering deep in thought. His eyes looked very worried now as he scanned around for a way out. The winds were now silent and stayed that way for a while, waiting patiently for his next move.

After my ears stopped ringing I asked Tianaju, "Where did he get the fire from?"

She answered, "All I can think of is, he must have also been swallowing up sunbeams. He is the most powerful form of energy that I have ever seen. If we had left it any later he would have been indestructible."

The dragon paced around and said, "Okay I'll make a deal with you. If you give me Tianaju's wand

I'll let you live. Now what do you say girls, eh I mean, dear friends?"

"No deal, dear sneaky, snowy one," replied the East Wind.

The dragon was almost white now bar for a circle of black and red in the middle of his chest.

"Well, if that's the way you want it, hold on to your nappies boys."

He coiled himself into a spring like form and hurtled down towards the sons, blasting them into the trees with what looked like his last blast of fiery thunder and lightning. Soaker and Toaster ripped through more of the trees, breaking them like carrots. At the same time the dragon followed them, and escaped through the path that they had created. He was away and traveling with great speed before the winds knew what had happened

Some of the trees were burning now from the last sheet of lightning. The North Wind waited until the sons had recovered, then told his brother the South Wind, "Quick put out the fires."

He turned to Howler telling him, "Hurry son, fetch Welusa and follow us. The dragon is heading south so be as quick as you can. We need to catch him before he gains more power."

Howler circled to see where I was and dived down to pick me up.

Tianaju shouted out, "Welusa, I am coming with you."

She jumped onto my back just in time before Howler picked me up.

Lianga shouted from underneath the bridge, "Don't' worry about me, I will be okay. See you later, and good luck Welusa."

As quick as a cannon goes bang, we were in the air, chasing after all the winds except for the South Wind. He was steadily putting out the forest fire and the ones in the village.

We traveled through the sky at a speed that you could not imagine. I couldn't see a thing and was getting bombarded by twigs, leaves and all sorts of flying objects. I was just about to cover my face with my hands when I suddenly realised I couldn't feel Tianaju on my back any more.

I shouted, "Tianaju, Tianaju."

I was just beginning to say where are you, when I got a poke in my chest and my pocket started tingling.

I said to myself, "The crafty little fairy, she's nice and snug in my pocket while I'm out here getting battered."

It seemed for ever before we caught up with the pursuing winds. In fact when we did, we found that they had caught the dragon and were now circling him. He was spitting out what looked like the last of his flaming energy. Howler set me down on a hill next to a pond. I looked around and realised I was beside the Keepers Pond, above my home town of Afon Llwyd.

Tianaju hopped out of my pocket and in a flash was standing beside me looking up at the dragon.

"It looks like he has lost all his power now. But be careful Welusa, he can still be dangerous. You can never know what he's capable of doing next," she warned me.

I shook all the leaves, twigs and everything else out of my hair and off my clothes, then stood and watched the snarling dragon.

The South Wind came blowing in and took up his position with the rest of the winds. There was a deathly silence now as the winds carefully watched Ohibronoeler. Finally it was the dragon that broke the silence saying, "Well come on then! It's all over ladies, you will never catch me."

He then took a deep breath, exhaled and disappeared. The winds stayed there but moved closer towards one another. It was like they were expecting this to happen.

Tianaju told me, "He is still there but he has dispersed into tiny specks of water. I can see him but you and the winds cannot, but they know he is there."

The great North Wind roared out a command saying, "Now, brother."

Then, the South Wind breathed out his wet breath all over the centre of the circle. Slowly, I began to see the shape of the dragon again. The very moment the winds could see him the North Wind gave another command, "Now! All of us together let's finish it."

Before I could say a word, they began blowing in sequence racing around the dragon at speed. This made him spin like a swirling spinning top. They continued spinning him until the North Wind shouted, "STOP!"

The dragon was clearly visible now and looked very dizzy. The winds then closed in squeezing him in the middle. The North and East Wind quickly breathed their cold and icy breath all over him. As I watched I could see the dragon was now slowly frosting up. My heart was thumping in my chest now and my throat was so dry I couldn't speak. Howler came down and said, "Come on Welusa! We have got him."

I looked at Tianaju and she smiled her beautiful smile and said, "It's up to you now."

I removed the pouch from my pocket and took out her lovely wavy lock of hair. I stooped down and picked up a small pebble and tucked it underneath the green ribbon the lock was tied with.

Howler then picked me up and carried me just above the middle of the frosted dragon. I took a few deep breaths, kissed her lovely lock of hair and dropped it down towards the centre of the dragon.

As I watched it floating down, the whole of my experience, from the time I was eight, up until the minute this was happening, flashed through my mind. A soon as the lock of hair made contact with the dragon there was a tremendous roar of pain. Howler backed away and so did all the other winds.

The dragon was now spitting and snarling as he writhed and swirled, twisting over and over. He was now glowing red as if he was about to explode. Then there was an almighty clap of thunder. I shut my eyes and when I opened them I saw a fabulous mass of flashing colour. It was orange, green and brown shooting across the sky line heading north to Scotland. I was then overjoyed as I saw millions upon millions of sparkling moonbeams racing their way back up to the moon. As soon as they hit the moon there was a big blue flash. I then caught sight of Ohibronoeler. He was now a real, live, small red dragon with tiny wings shouting out, "I'll get you Welusa."

I watched as he spiraled down and down, tumbling over and over struggling to fly until he splashed into a pond next to the Keepers Pond.

Howler set me down beside the pond and said, "Well done Welusa."

I replied, "Thank you Howler my dear friend."

The next thing I knew Tianaju was on my back with her arms around my neck kissing my head saying, "Thank you, Welusa. You have been magnificent. I will make it up to you I promise."

I turned my head and said, "It was the winds that did all the hard work. I just had the easy bit that's all. But it's all over now, so let's thank them shall we?"

As we know they could not see Tianaju so all I could do was to shout, "The Emerald Queen of Children thanks you with all her heart. She also thanks you on behalf of Fairyland. I myself would like to thank all you mighty winds for everything you have done for the world. I would especially like to thank Nipper for saving my life back in Scarborough and to Howler who gave me the ride of my life and made it possible for me to slay the dragon."

The North wind replied, "We thank the Emerald Queen of Children and you Welusa for saving our lives too. For without the moonbeams, we would have been weakened and would have surely died. We must say goodbye to you now and to the beautiful queen. We all have our work to do and must get back to it."

The mighty winds rose high in the air and with a lovely mighty roar, they soared away in different directions, except for Howler.

He swooped down and looked me in the eyes and said, "Ride of your life! Pah, that was just a spin in the dark sonny."

Before I knew it, he had picked me up and we were soaring high into the air. He stopped and asked me, "Are you ready boy?"

I replied, "Ready for what!"

"The ride of your life," he howled.

He held me in his arms and covered me with his fingers saying, "These will protect you, but you will still be able to see through them and breathe."

He then tore off heading towards Scotland. We sped along with incredible speed, looping up and over, zooming down to the ground and back up again. I was laughing with excitement as he twisted and turned his way through trees and buildings towards the North coast. The lovely sound of him howling along was just fabulous. I remember thinking to myself, "Wow, this is fantastic. Fancy me, being friends with the mighty Howler."

As we were approaching the cold Scottish coast, I saw that all the beautiful colours that had come from the dragon, were now wavering across the sky line. It looked to me as if they were waving for joy saying, "Look at us we are over here?"

When Howler saw the lights he slowed down and said, "Aurora Borealis"

I shouted, "What does that mean?"

He replied, "Just beautiful."

He then raced on and asked me, "Do you want to take a dip little warrior?"

I quickly replied, "No, no, not today thank you."

He replied, "What! Are you afraid of a drop of water? Well, we'll see about that."

We tore up into the air and dived back down towards the cold North Sea at a tremendous speed.

I held my breath and said to myself, "Oh no."

I was quickly relieved, because just before hitting the sea, he looped back up again laughing.

I laughed too and shouted, "That was a rotten trick Howler. I thought you were going to drop me in that freezing sea again."

He just laughed and headed back towards Wales. Once again we streaked through the sky at a speed faster than before. We looped the loop, twisted and turned all the way back to Wales.

As Howler set me down beside the Keepers Pond, I told him, "That was just amazing Howler."

He looked at me and said; "Now THAT'S what I call a ride sonny. See you later kid. I've got work to do."

Then, I saw him smile for the first time as he took off powering his way back to Scotland.

Tianaju hugged me again and said, "You are wonderful."

I looked at her and said, "Well if that's what you think, that makes two of us."

She then told me that following the blue flash all the coal dust and soot on the moon was sent hurtling down to Earth. It was now spread out over most of the Welsh hills and mountains.

I laughed and said, "Wow that means there is free coal for everyone now."

She smiled, held my hand and told me, "While you were away with Howler I went to fetch Lianga."

"Where is he?" I asked.

She replied, "He is over there by the pond watching the small dragon swimming around. I have put a magic circle around the pond so Ohibronoeler will never be able to get out. Perhaps in time if he changes his ways I will release him."

"Well, what are we going to do now?" I asked.

She answered, "Firstly you had better visit your parents. I should imagine they are wondering where you are."

I answered, "Well it's just down the road so I'll pop in and see them. Are you coming or are you off back home?"

She replied, "I will have to go back to my parents too, but I will be back for you. If you remember you promised to come with me to repay the kind people who helped us."

"Yes I remember," I said.

She kissed me on the cheek and said, "I will see you in three days."

She then looked up at the now lovely pure white moon and slowly disappeared into the night sky waving as she went.

I waited for a while until the sun began to rise, then said to Lianga, "Well pal, I'm off to see my Mam and Dad, they are usually getting up by now. We haven't got a stable so will you be alright up here?"

He replied, "Don't worry about me I will be fine. Give me a call if you need me."

I walked off down the hill leaving the dragon swimming around in his new home. My mother answered the door in her dressing gown and flung her arms around me saying, "It's lovely to see you son. Come in you must be freezing. Were you out in that terrible wind last night? I thought we were going to be blown away."

My father gave me a hug as I walked in, saying, "I have just lit the fire Welusa, go and warm yourself up. I am off to work now, so I'll see you later, Son."

I sat down in the nice comfy armchair, looking at the flickering hypnotizing fire and fell fast asleep. When I awoke, my mother was sat opposite me smiling.

"Come on; get those clothes off and into the bath. It's all ready for you," she said.

I sat there soaking in the bath until it began to chill. My mother had set out some nice clean clothes for me on my soft bed. This made me feel nice and clean again wearing fresh new clothes. I felt great.

I led on my bed thinking, "It's a waste of time telling anyone about this extraordinary mission. They will never believe me."

So later that evening, I sat around the fire, chatting with my Mam and Dad.

"Well, how did you get on Welusa? My mother asked. "You have been away for a while, so you must have found work somewhere. Tell me, what sort of job is it?"

I replied, "Yes I did find work. It was tough, but I enjoyed it. Unfortunately it has now come to an end, I have had the sack."

My mother exclaimed, "What!"

I laughed and said, "I am only kidding. I found a job delivering messages. I had a horse of my own and it's been great fun riding him all around the country. I can only stay for a few days. I have to go back on Friday."

"Who is the lady friend?" asked my mother.

I replied, "What lady friend?"

She replied, "Well if you haven't got a lady friend, you must be splashing perfume on yourself. Now come on, you can't fool me, what's her name?"

I acted as if it slipped my memory and replied, "Oh yes, she is not my lady friend as such. I just work for her, but she is also a good friend."

"Oh yes, I bet she is," my mother said in disbelief.

"Leave the lad be, Sarah," said my father as he winked at me.

"Well come on, what's her name then?" she insisted.

I didn't want to tell a lie so I had to think for a minute and replied, "Juanita, her name is Juanita."

"That's a nice name," she said. "It means the grace of God. It's also the meaning to the name of the fairy queen in your book. So are you kidding me again Welusa?"

My father interrupted saying, "Of course he is. Leave him alone woman," and winked at me again."

He then changed the subject and asked, "Where is your horse son?"

I answered, "He's grazing up on the hill. I will show you him tomorrow. He is a fine horse dad, you will like him."

"Okay I'll check him over. Well it's time for bed now son, I have to get up in the morning for work."

I didn't sleep well that night. With all the flying, and the fearsome battle, it made me restless. It felt as if I had only been asleep for five minutes before the song thrush started whistling and woke me up. I heard my mother and father go downstairs, so I got dressed and had a cup of tea and some toast with them. I then walked with my father up to Kay's Slope coal mine, which was two miles away, in the village of Garn-yr-erw. All the miners have to walk quite a long way through an underground tunnel, before they finally reach the coal face.

I left him at the entrance and said, "See you later Dad." I watched as he walked with his mates, down the tunnel and disappear into the darkness.

I looked over to the Milfraen Mountain and decided because I had nothing much to do that day I would take a walk up to the top. So I set off along the path past the old Whistle Inn. The Whistle is where the miners sometimes call in for a jar of ale after work. Cliff, the Town Crier, who is also the Whistle's friendly landlord, was outside stacking empty barrels and waved as I passed. After I reached the top of the mountain I sat on a rock looking down the lovely valley. It was a clear day so I could see the Bristol Channel quite clearly. Down below was the recently closed Milfraen Colliery. I could see children playing behind the six coal board houses. It looked as if they were playing ring a ring a roses around a tall solitary tree. I was sat there thinking about the book I was going to write when I noticed that all across the Garn- yr- erw Mountain was black.

I said to myself, "That must be some of the soot and coal dust from the moon."

I was so deep in thought that I didn't notice the mountain fog coming down behind me.

So I began to make my way back down but the fog came down so quick and thick that I strayed completely off the path. All I could do was head towards the sound of the horses pulling the coal trams from the mine. I was beginning to get very worried until I heard Cliff. He was practicing crying out the news, not far from me. So I headed for the sound of his loud voice and got down safe enough.

I went home and took out my journal, that I had written nearly every day of my mission, and started work on it. I began turning my notes into the full story of my amazing adventure with Tianaju and the lock of her hair. Later on, about five o'clock, I collected Lianga and thought I would treat my dad to a ride home from work. He was surprised to see me and instantly loved Lianga.

"Wow son, this is the finest horse I've ever seen."

As we trotted home he told me that all the men were talking about the small coal and dust across the mountain. They were all baffled as to where it came from. He enjoyed the ride home that day and so did I. My mother also fell in love with Lianga and gave him a good brush down before I let him off to graze.

Later I met up with my pals, who I hadn't seen for months, and went for a walk up Llanover road as far as the mountain well. We had a great time joking with one another and throwing rocks. Although I had been away for a while I still finished up being the champion thrower. My pals mentioned to me about the moon being so dark lately. They all thought it was some kind of long eclipse. I told them that it must be okay now because it was bright again last night.

I then joked, "It must have been covered in coal because it's all over the mountains now."

They laughed and said, "Yeah, you never know, because it certainly came from somewhere."

We stayed there until twilight then we all headed home. I did some more work on my story before I climbed into bed. I was so worn out from throwing those rocks that I went to sleep almost immediately.

In the morning I walked my father to work again. On my way back through Garn-yr-erw village I thought I'd take a short cut up between the coal tips and over the newly coal covered mountain to look for Lianga. I found him grazing near the Keepers pond again. He told me that he was okay, so I thought I would check on the dragon. As I approached his pond, I saw just a glimpse of him before he dived down hiding in the bottom. I left him there stirring up the mud and went down town to the Friday market. I spent a good part of the day wandering around before I went home for my six o'clock evening meal. While I was in town that day all everyone was talking about was the dark moon, the coal dust and the terrible storm the other night.

Veronica Rolph told me that the receded sea had rushed back into the Swansea shores flooding the whole area, even the market. Dozens of massive rocks were washed up onto the Mumbles beach and loads more were scattered all around the coast.

After my meal, I went up to my bedroom to write some more of my story. I was enjoying myself writing away until my mother shouted, "Welusa! There is someone at the door for you."

I hid my story in the same place where I had hidden the lock of hair. I ran down stairs and to my delightful surprise it was Tianaju. She was standing in the doorway smiling and dressed for traveling. "Are you ready?" she asked.

I replied, "I will be very shortly. Come in, it won't take me long."

She came in and I introduced her saying, "Mam, Dad, this is Juanita."

I turned to Tianaju and winked at her saying, "Juanita, this is my parents."

My parents were amazed as she took down her hood. They were so shocked with how lovely she was that they couldn't speak. So I asked her, "Would you like to sit down by the fire? I will just fetch my bag."

I ran upstairs and back down again before my parents could ask her too many questions.

"Right, I will just put my boots on and we'll be on our way," I shouted.

As I was out in the hall putting my boots on, my mother came up to me asking,

"Is this beautiful girl really your boss or are you still kidding me, Welusa?"

I answered, "She is not a girl, she is a lady. I know what you are thinking, Mam. But no, she isn't my girlfriend as such. She really is my boss and also a good friend."

At that point, Tianaju came into the hall and asked me to bring two of my books with me. I dashed back up stairs and got them. We then said goodbye to my mother and father and walked off up the Keepers Hill. Lianga came trotting down to meet us pulling a lovely two toned green coach.

"Wow!" I said. "It's fabulous. So we are off again with a lovely new coach. How long will it take us this time?"

She replied, "It will take as long as you like. I have given Lianga the magic to run as fast as you ask him to. He can also fly now so you can fly by night, gallop or walk by day. It's entirely up to you."

I was overjoyed, so the first thing I asked was, "Where are we going to first?"

She answered, "How about Ragged Castle."

"Oh yes, it will be nice to see my pals again," I replied excitedly.

"Well let's go there then, but first I have money for all our needs," she said and smiled.

So off we went down over the other side of Keepers hill, around the sharp corner we call the Fiddlers Elbow, then on through Abergavenny town heading eastward across Wales.

The following evening we stopped just outside the little village of Hay on Wye.

"We will stay in the village for the night. There is no need for us to camp any more. Come Welusa, let's just take Lianga and find an Inn," said the happy queen.

She then waved her wand and the lovely coach vanished into thin air.

When we arrived at the village we found that it was the last day of a week-long music and art festival. Tianaju gave me some money to look for an Inn, and a livery stable. I left her with Lianga in the village square while I went away to search. I found the perfect place overlooking the river Wye. There was only one room available but fortunately for us it had two beds, so I was lucky. The Inn also had nice stables around the back.

When I came back, I found Tianaju sitting down alongside a young artist. He was drawing a charcoal portrait of Lianga.

She smiled and introduced me to him saying, "This is Scott Gallear from Pontypwl. He liked Lianga so much that I asked him to draw his portrait for you."

When he had finished she thanked him and gave him two gold coins.

"Wow! Thank you so much," he gratefully said. Then he skipped his way down the street shouting, "Awesome, just awesome."

The drawing was fabulous. Tianaju gently rolled it up and gave it to me. I thanked her and put it safely away in my bag.

I patted Lianga and said, "Come on, let's take you around to the stables."

We left him there munching a bowl of fresh oats and nice sweet hay. We headed back through the village and booked a meal in the Swan Tavern which was situated at the end of the main street.

It was the first proper meal we had eaten for a long time. It was delicious, so to round off a perfect day we took a walk along the banks of the river Wye. There were about a dozen fishermen there fishing for trout, so we decided to watch them for a while. We then walked on and as we did so, I saw a flash in the shallow part of the river. Exactly where the flash had occurred was a silvery pouch lying in the water close to the bank.

"That must have something to do with you," I said as I went over to investigate.

I picked the pouch out of the river and found to my amazement that it was full of gold nuggets.

"Wow! You must have put these there. What are they for?" I asked.

She replied, "They are for all the kind people who helped us and gave us shelter. You can tell them that you had found gold in a river. That way you will not be telling any lies."

I laughed and said, "They are going to have some big surprise. You are a very clever little queen Tianaju, aren't you?"

We sat down on a bench and watched the fishermen until dusk, then walked back to the Inn.

Before we went to our room we waited for the Inn keeper to make us our usual jug of hot milk.

While we were sitting on our beds, Tianaju talked nonstop. It seemed as if she was expecting something special to happen. We talked on until we were tired and ready for sleep. She changed into her nightwear with a wave of her wand, and climbed into her bed. I blew out the candle, changed and climbed into mine. I slept well until I got tipped out onto the floor by the laughing queen.

"Wakey wakey. Come on, up you get, it's morning," she said.

"I'll get you for that," I promised her.

She replied, "You can try. Come on let's have some breakfast and head on to Ragged Castle."

I threw a pillow at her and said, "That sounds great."

We traveled on after breakfast for another two days. As we drove along, the wheels seemed as if they were skimming over the ground, because I couldn't feel any bumps. It was just like we were flying but still on the ground. It was six o'clock in the evening when we arrived at the castle. My pal Lord Rabry was just coming around the corner and was happy to see us again.

"Great to see you again Welusa, I was hoping you'd come back. We are not long in from town and I have just put my horse and trap away. Put your horse in the stable and go on in, the both of you. I'll go and fetch some logs. I won't be long."

Lady Meryl was also pleased to see us as she welcomed us in saying "It's lovely to see you again Welusa and you too Evely. Go on in and sit by the fire. I'll warm up something nice to eat."

Tianaju sat down by the fire and I went out to help my pal carry in the logs.

After we had eaten and cleared away the dishes, we sat around the fire. As we chatted I decided it was an ideal time to tell them of my good fortune.

I explained to them, "On our journey across Wales I found gold in a river. It was more than enough for any one person. So, my dear friends, we would like you to accept four nuggets as a token of our friendship."

They were both over whelmed and couldn't stop thanking us. Lord Rabry was so happy that he fetched a fiddle for me and a homemade penny whistle for himself. I played quite a few tunes while Lord Rabry tried his best. The girls had a great time and danced until they were exhausted.

My old mate threw the whistle away and said, "I hate that whistle. Well that's me finished I'm off to bed."

"Yes, me too," I said.

So we wished each other good night and went to our rooms. I didn't bother getting into bed because I knew I wouldn't be in there for long. So I led on the rug and waited. It wasn't long before I heard a plonk on the bed and Tianaju saying, "Good night."

I replied, "Yeah, sleep well."

In the morning after breakfast we bid goodbye to our happy friends and headed once more to Scotland.

We trotted along for a while then I asked Tianaju, "If I wanted to fly tonight how would I do it?"

She replied, "Just ask Lianga."

I thought a while and said, "Perhaps I will give it a try tonight then."

We sped on, stopping every now and then for a snack and a rest.

As soon as it was dark, I asked Lianga, "Is it okay to try out a spot of flying now?"

He answered, "I have been waiting for you to ask me that. So come on what are we waiting for, let's fly."

I tapped him on his tail and said, "Okay let's fly to York first and if we like it we'll carry on to Hawick."

He looked up and sprang with ease into the air. We sailed through the night sky just like Santa Claus. It was sensational, in fact it was so exhilarating that I shouted, "Don't bother stopping at York Lianga, head on to Hawick."

He answered, "Aye, aye Cap'n."

So we fled through the warm night, laughing and joking, until we landed just outside Hawick in the borders of Scotland. It was too late to book a room so we slept in the coach. It rained all night and most of the morning. In the afternoon we decided to stay for another night so I booked a room over a tavern with two beds. We found a stable for Lianga and decided to take a walk around the town. As we walked over the bridge into town we were surprised to see Enda the juggler running towards us. As he passed by, there was a terrible smell, he was covered in tomatoes, and what must have been rotten eggs. He was being chased out of town by a crowd shouting, "Get out and don't come back. You are the worst juggler we have ever seen."

In the middle of the town there was an impressive looking town hall. It had a fine tall tower with a clock that was just striking three o'clock. The locals told us that it was built two years ago and that it was the pride of the town. The sun was shining again so it was nice browsing around the market for the rest of the afternoon. I was hungry now and looking forward to our evening meal. After the meal we went to bed as we wanted to make an early start.

As the cock crowed the next morning we set off to Dunkeld to check on the damage. Between galloping and flying, we arrived there at about five o'clock the next day. The villagers were busy repairing their houses and the builders were working on the Cathedral. We paid for two rooms in the same Inn we stayed in two weeks ago. The Landlady told us that part of their roof had been blown off during a terrible storm the night we had left and that it had also demolished the lovely stables so there was nowhere for Lianga to stay. This being the case we headed through the village and down to the river. I unhitched Lianga and with a puff of Tianaju's magic, the coach disappeared. Lianga told us that he was okay because he liked it there by the river.

I looked over to what used to be a lovely forest and saw that the broken trees were being cut up into small logs. They were probably for all the village folk to use as fire wood.

Tianaju suggested, "Tomorrow we must find a way to give these people some of our gold to help them with repairs."

I replied, "Well, one way is to leave some in the Cathedral collection box. Another way is to give some to the local council. As for the town folk perhaps you can think of something."

"Good idea Welusa, and yes I will think of something," she said as we walked back to the Inn.

That night after a quick night cap Tianaju suggested, "Come on, it's time for another early night."

I lay there on my bed waiting for her to come in as usual, but I fell asleep. In the morning when I awoke I found that I was still on the bed. There was no sign of Tianaju anywhere. I lay there for a while until I heard the Landlady's little girl shouting,

"I saw the Emerald Queen of Children last night. She told me a lovely story about herself and look Mammy she gave me some gold?"

I then realised that she had been busy all night. I dressed and knocked on her door. She opened it and told me to come in.

I asked, "Where were you last night?"

She replied, "I have to be invisible now, just until we are out of town. I have visited every child in the village and told them my life story. I gave them all two nuggets of gold each for their parents. I also used a little bit of magic to repair all the damage to their homes and buildings. So all you will have to do now is to leave some gold in the Cathedral's collection box."

I told her that was fine but we had better hurry. She then disappeared with her bag as I crept downstairs and out the door before anyone saw me. They were all too busy discussing what had happened during the night to notice me leaving on my own. The whole village was buzzing with excitement. They just couldn't believe what the Queen had done for them all, and that they were now rich. I walked off to the Cathedral and found that too was back to its original state. The workers were just stood there in amazement. So as they were all talking to one another I slipped inside and put two gold nuggets into the Cathedral's fund box then slipped back out again. As I came out Lianga was around the corner hitched up waiting for me. As I climbed up Tianaju suddenly reappeared and was sitting beside me smiling that beautiful smile again.

As we trotted out of town I was surprised to see that even the forest down by the river had been restored. Every tree was there again and even the leaves had changed colour.

I looked at her, gently shook my head and said, "You are just amazing. You have done a wonderful job but you've missed a bit of straw on one of the cottages."

She laughed and said, "Your nose is getting longer every day."

As we trotted happily along she asked me, "Can you get the two books ready?"

I answered, "Yes okay. What do you want them for?"

She pointed ahead and said, "Chris, the tramp from Canada, is on this road ahead of us. You can sign the books and give them to him for his grandchildren."

About a mile further on, we saw him sat on the roadside.

I stopped opposite him and said, "Hello there Chris. You have come a fair way since we saw you last. How was the cabin?"

He answered in a surprised voice, "Oh, it's you again. Good morning to you both. Yes I have come a long way. I have been very fortunate with many lifts and yes, the cabin was great. It reminded me of the days when I was young."

I stepped down from the coach and handed him the two books saying, "These two books are for your Grandnippers. We would like you to have them."

He thanked us both and said, "I will keep them safe. It will probably be twelve months before I reach Canada, but I am sure they will be overjoyed with such a present. I'll probably be the best Grandpapa ever now."

We left him there on the side of the road. Then for some strange reason, he rolled a stone down the road and said, "This could be the last time, I don't know."

I shouted out as we went, "By the way, you can tell the nips that you have just been talking to the beautiful queen that's in their books."

We laughed and galloped away heading further north to Priscilla's lodge in Killie Crankie. It was a nice sunny day so we just took our time and trotted along. The following day, as we were nearing the lodge, we met Cilla just arriving home with her donkey and cart. She was on her way back from town and was very pleased to see us again. Tianaju handed her two nuggets of gold, wrapped up in a purse, saying, "This is just a little present to show our appreciation for your kindness."

Priscilla replied, "Thank you both, now if you wait until I have seen to the donkey and cart, we will have some tea and you can stay the night."

Tianaju gratefully said, "Thank you for your kind offer but we really must be on our way."

She replied, "That's a shame but you are welcome to stay any time you are passing."

We said our goodbyes and hurried off before she opened her present.

I joked with Tianaju saying, "She'll get a lovely surprise when she opens it. Perhaps she will buy the whole shop the next time she goes shopping."

We traveled on until it was dark. I waited a while before I asked Lianga, "Will it be alright with you if we fly the rest of the way to Carrbridge?"

"Yahoo! with pleasure Welusa," he replied

We soared off into the night sky like a bird flying home to his nest. We arrived just outside Carrbridge and camped there for the night. We were up early in the morning watching the beautiful sun slowly rising from behind the hill. It was midday before we trotted off to Patricia and Stuart's cottage. When we arrived there they were both at home and happy to see us.

"It's lovely to see you again. We are just about to have our lunch, so come in and join us."

We joined them for some lovely homemade bread and a bowl of soup.

"That was lovely," I said. "Now we have something lovely for you too. On our travels I was lucky enough to find gold in a river. There is more than enough for Tianaju and me. So we would like you to accept these four gold nuggets to show you our appreciation of your kindness towards us."

They were both astounded, but delighted. Patricia told us that they needed a new roof on their cottage, and a new pony and trap. They were so excited that they hugged us dearly.

It was a nice feeling as we waved goodbye knowing that they were happy.

Our next destination was Inverness and on to Brother Martin's Monastery. On our way there, we stopped in some woods, and while we were there, a golden eagle, called Dorothy, visited us saying, "Zilo the wolf, that attacked you near Inverness, is deeply sorry and would like to apologise to you personally Welusa."

I thanked the fabulous eagle and told her to tell Zilo that we will stop in the same woods as before. She then stretched her enormous wings and flew slowly away into the clear blue sky. We headed off, taking our time and stopped once again in the same woodland where the wolf attacked me. I lit a fire and Tianaju boiled some potatoes and vegetables. It was not long after our meal was cooked, that Zilo the wolf came walking into camp. He had his head down low as if in shame.

"I am very sorry, Welusa, for attacking you. I had no other choice because Ohibronoeler, the Dragon, told me that you were a Sorcerer and was going to kill my baby cubs. I didn't know you were with the Emerald Queen of Children. Can you please forgive me?"

I patted him on his head and consoled him saying, "Yes, I will forgive you Zilo, and to prove it, you can join us for supper. We haven't got any meat but I do have a nice bowl of milk for dessert,"

We shared out our meal and had a nice long chat until dark.

Zilo promised me before he left, that I would never be attacked by any Scottish wolf again.

I stroked him and said, "Thank you and I wish you and your family well."

Tianaju waved her wand and gave him six nice bones for his wife and babies. He carried them off between his broken teeth and disappeared into the dark woods.

After washing up the dishes, we washed our hands and face, climbed into the coach and went sound asleep.

In the morning we decided to visit the town of Inverness. Our plan was to walk around the town until dark then fly to Brother Martin's Monastery, and camp outside until the following morning.

Tianaju pointed her hand towards the coach and it disappeared.

I was curious so I asked her, "I thought you had to use your wand."

She answered, "No, I just have to have it with me."

We rode Lianga into town and found that there was a carnival going on. So that was fun to watch. There was a huge selection of people, parading through the town, dressed up as different characters. There were also clowns, acrobats, tall men walking on stilts, and gypsy fortune tellers. The festival lasted until late afternoon and by that time everyone were worn out. Then to our surprise as the crowds began to clear, we saw Brother Martin with Brother James walking on the opposite side of the street.

"Hello Brother Martin," I shouted.

He looked over to us and said, "Well, my word, it's the young lad with the injured arm, and the bonnie wee lassie."

We walked over to them and sat down on a bench.

He asked me, "How is your arm lad? Did you deliver your message?"

I replied, "Yes we did deliver the message, and my arm is fine now thanks to you. We were just coming to see you, because before we go back home we have something to give you. You were so kind to us both, especially me with my injured arm, that we would like you to accept a small gift for your Monastery."

Tianaju gave him four gold nuggets inside a leather pouch and told him not to open it until we were gone. He agreed and was very grateful for the gift and gave us his blessing before we left.

"Well, Tianaju, that's them all. Where are we going now?"

She replied, "I think we should wait until dark Welusa, then, fly back to Hawick for the last time."

I was happy now and said, "Okay. I am beginning to like this flying."

"Me too," said Lianga, as he whinnied with joy.

Off we trotted out of town heading for where we had camped. When we reached there, I was surprised to see a nice burning fire with a pot simmering away on it.

"It's my own special fairy broth," Tianaju told me.

"Wow! That's handy." I said, looking at the pot. "This magic is great. I hope there's a nice cream cake for dessert?"

She laughed and replied, "No it's not your birthday yet."

She then waved her wand and the coach appeared from nowhere. Lianga wandered off into the woods, while we sat down and enjoyed Tianaju's lovely fairy broth. Later as we were sitting around the fire I said, "Well, that's us finished now. One more night and we are home. It's been some adventure Tianaju."

She told me once again, "I'll make it up to you."

I replied, "There is no need to make it up to me. If the dragon had not been stopped, the whole world would have suffered. I am just so happy that you told me about him and that I was able to help."

"Well in that case I am so happy that you did. Come on Welusa; let's fly to Hawick for the night."

I replied, "Great, but on the way, I want to stop in Dunkeld for an hour. There is something that I want to do first."

She called Lianga and he came in shaking himself. He got very excited when I told him that we were about to head on. We hitched him up, and flew into the night sky heading south again. As we flew above the clouds I could hear him shouting, "Weeee!" He absolutely loved it and so did I!

As we sailed along Tianaju pointed to the stars and said, "See those two stars over there to the east."

I answered, "Yes, I see them."

"Well they are called Gemini, and Gemini is my birth sign."

I looked at her and asked, "Wow! Do I have a birth sign?"

She replied, "Sadly, no. You were born on the twenty ninth of February in a leap year. No one born in a leap year has a birth sign."

I looked at the stars and said to her disappointedly, "Oh! That's a shame. Fancy that. I'm the only one without a birth sign." I then jokingly asked her, "Do you think you could make one for me?"

She laughed and nudged me saying, "I'm only kidding, that's your stars up there. Do you see the clump of stars that looks like a wiggly fish? They are called Pisces, and Pisces is your birth sign."

I nudged her back and said, "Oh, you little joker."

As we sailed through the sky she pointed out all the twelve signs of the Zodiac. It was fascinating listening to her describing all the shapes to me.

As we approached Dunkeld I asked Lianga to set down on our favourite spot by the river. We climbed down from the coach and went for a walk through the woods. We made our way to a huge spreading oak tree that had survived the epic battle.

It was one of many that Tianaju didn't need to restore. This may seem strange to you but I looked up at the lovely tree and asked him would it be okay if I carved our names in his trunk. He told me he would consider it to be a great honour. Tianaju's wand was shining nicely and the last quarter moon was out, so I took out my knife and carved our names on the tree's broad trunk.

The queen hugged my arm and said, "That was a lovely thing to do. Our names will be there forever."

I nudged her and said, "I'll race you back to the coach but no cheating."

She replied okay and we got on our marks. I can tell you now even without her wings and magic she was twice as fast as me. She was stood there waiting by the coach as I was climbing over the stile by the bridge.

She shouted, "Come on you slow coach. Where have you been?"

As I ran up to her I tripped over one of those dreaded mole hills again.

She burst out laughing saying, "Oh, you are all dirty."

I picked her up and carried her to the river and said, "Well maybe we had better have a wash then."

She squealed, "Don't you dare Welusa."

I put her down and said, "Well I might. You put that mole hill there on purpose didn't you?"

She giggled and said, "Well I might have." Then ran away laughing.

It was no use running after her so I laughed and shouted, "Come on back. I promise I'm not going to throw you in the river." Then I said to myself, "Well, not tonight anyway."

She came back still laughing, and I was laughing too.

We climbed up onto the coach, said goodbye to Dunkeld and soared into the half moonlit, starry night sky, heading for Hawick.

After arriving at a little village called Denholm, which is a few miles outside of Hawick, we camped alongside the River Teviot. It was peaceful there with just the rippling sound of running water to send us fast asleep.

Early the next morning we trotted off towards Hawick. On the way, we passed Fatlips Castle and I noticed that there was a poster at the end of the drive. It was advertising a masked ball in the town hall that night.

Tianaju was excited and said, "We must go to this ball. It should be fun."

We arrived in Hawick and bought a few bits and pieces for our last journey down to Wales the following morning. There were posters everywhere advertising the masked ball. This made Tianaju even more excited because she had never been to one before. Neither had I.

"Yippee!" she shouted. "I can't wait to go there tonight."

I asked her, "What are we going to wear?"

She replied, "I'll think of something but I hope you are feeling fit because I love to dance all night. Come on let's go back to Denholm and book a room for the night."

We headed back to Denholm and paid for two rooms in a lovely wee Inn called The Auld Cross

Keys. Lianga was happy to go wandering down by the river.

The landlord asked, "What part of the country are you from?"

"Wales," I told him.

"Dear me, you have come a long way. What brings you here lad?"

I thought a while and said, "We are friends with King Logan and we are going to the masked ball."

"Ah well done laddie it will be a grand night, I am sure you will enjoy it. I will give you a key to come in whenever you like. Anyone who is a friend of King Logan, is a friend of mine."

He showed us to our rooms and said, "There is no need to have an evening meal because there will be plenty of haggis and tatties to eat at the ball."

I lay down on my bed for an hour or two listening to the village news teller shouting out the news. Later, Tianaju came into my room and asked me to stand up. I stood up, facing her, while she waved her tiny wand and showered me with rainbows again. When they disappeared, I found that I was dressed like a posh highlander in red tartan. I looked in the mirror and saw that my beard had grown into a long one, so I explained to her, "I'll be scratching all night with this."

"Oh, that's a shame," she said disappointedly. "But I suppose you are right."

She pointed her wand at my long beard and it went back to normal again.

"That's better," I said. "I only like my beard short. What are you wearing? Where's your mask?"

"Here it is," she told me as a purple coloured mask appeared in her hand.

"Ho, ho," I laughed. But what are you wearing? Are you going to wear your riding clothes?"

Then, just as quick as I could blink my eye, she was dressed like a Scottish lady, wearing a purple jacket with silver buttons, a white blouse, a purple tartan skirt, socks to match and shiny purple shoes.

"Well what do you think?" she asked.

I sighed, held her hands and replied, "You look simply wonderful. You are so beautiful. If you were not a fairy I would, uh, I would uh, oh never mind, I forgot what I was going to say now. Come on, let's go to the ball."

She pushed me back onto the bed and said, "Oh you! What? What would you do or say if I wasn't a fairy?"

I rolled over and got off the other side, crossed my fingers and said, "Oh, it just slipped my mind. As I was looking at you a fly went in my eye and I forgot what I was going to say. Besides, whatever it was, it was probably ridiculous anyway."

She huffed and said once again, "Oh you! Come on then, let's get Lianga."

We collected Lianga and set off for Hawick which was about eight miles away. When we arrived, after stepping down from the coach, she put on her mask, sprinkled some magic and once again the coach vanished.

Lianga shook himself down, "See you later. Don't worry about me, Welusa, just enjoy yourselves. Call me when you're ready, your Highness," he said as he trotted up into the hills.

As we made our way through the town we were greeted by King Logan's hound. He recognised us immediately and pulled his handler across the road to meet us.

"Hello your Majesty. Are you coming to stay with us again?" he asked.

She bent down and whispered in his ear, "No. I am sorry Joshua, but we are staying in Denholm for the night and then heading back home tomorrow, but it is lovely to see you again. Now, we must go before we are late for the ball."

We left him to drag his handler back across the street while we headed for the town hall. The ball was free to enter as long as the ladies were wearing a mask. Tianaju wore a purple sparkling one that just covered her eyes. Men had the option to wear masks, but I chose not to. I couldn't help feeling proud walking into the hall with such a beautiful woman on my arm. Although Tianaju was wearing a mask she still drew gasps from the crowd as we made our way inside, searching for a seat on the side of the dance floor.

We had only just found a seat when the trumpets sounded and the herald announced the arrival of the king. We all bowed and curtsied as King Logan and his sons entered the hall. The king stood up on the stage and to everyone's delight, said, "Let the ball begin."

Everyone cheered and shouted, "Long live King Logan."

He clapped his hands and said, "Let the music begin. Come, everyone dance, enjoy yourselves."

The band began to play and we all lined up for a dance they called a reel. The reel wasn't easy because you changed partners every now and then. So, most of the time, I changed the wrong one, but

I soon improved as the night went on. Tianaju loved the new dance and it was hard work trying to get her to sit down to have a rest. When the band announced that they were having a break, I said to myself as we sat down, "Thank goodness for that."

All the food and drink was free so I went to fetch some mugs of lemonade. It took a while, because as you can imagine there was a long queue. The band began playing again just as it was my turn in the queue. So, when I came back, Tianaju was surrounded by a few young men. One of them was holding her arm trying to get her up to dance. Then, someone roared out "STOP!"

It was the king. The band stopped and everyone stood still. He then pointed to the young man that had now loosed go of Tianaju's arm, and told him, "GO! Be on your way home lad."

The man left the hall with his head down low. The band started playing again and by this time I was alongside her with the refreshing drinks. As we sat there enjoying the rest, a smiling Prince Scott approached us saying, "Greetings to you both. My father recognised you the moment you had your first dance. He would like you to come and join us at our table."

We accepted his invitation and followed the prince.

"Welcome, Welusa and you too Tianaju. Come, sit beside me the both of you," said the delighted king.

He then looked at Tianaju and said, "My word lassie, you need more than a mask covering your eyes my dear."

He then laughed and added, "In fact you need a hood and a full mask to hide that beautiful face of yours. My advice to you, my pretty one, is get yourself married and put a ring on your finger. Otherwise you will be pestered for the rest of your life."

She blushed and answered, "Thank you great King for your kind advice."

"You are very welcome, my sweet lass. Now come, I feel like dancing, so let's all dance."

He then shouted to the band, "Liven it up lads, and play me the best reels you know. Yahoo! I'm ready to dance the night away."

Everyone was amazed and laughed with excitement as the king lined up for the reel. He made a point of dancing with every lady in the room. It was a fabulous evening. We couldn't have wished for a more enjoyable end to our time in bonnie Scotland.

It wasn't the end though. As we were saying our goodbyes to the king, he insisted that we attend the games that were being held the next day. We could not refuse.

There was such a buzz as we all walked home through the town chatting to one another. It was a lovely night, so we decided to walk awhile before calling Lianga.

As we walked, I couldn't help thinking about what the king had said to Tianaju. So I asked her if she had ever thought about getting married.

She answered, "I have, and there is something that I have to say to you Welusa, but I will wait until we get back to Wales."

"Okay," I said.

We walked on until we came alongside a bridge over the river and then she called Lianga. Within a few minutes he came trotting along, pulling the coach behind him. We trotted slowly back to Denholm and went to our rooms. As usual, in about ten minutes, I was back on the floor and Tianaju was in my bed, but she was kind enough to bring me her mattress.

The next day after lunch we headed into Hawick for the start of the games. We decided to ride Lianga and not to take the coach. When we arrived, King Logan invited us to join his party. We watched as he fired off a loud cannon to open the games. The games were held in a large field alongside the River Teviot. Foot racing was one of the main sports of the day and it was very exciting to witness. The field was marked out in a straight, one hundred yard race to the line. The runners were all shapes and sizes and they all raced in heats to reach the final. It made me feel out of breath just watching them. There were all kinds of entertaining games going on at the same time. Most of them I had never seen before. The final of the foot race was very close and was won by a local lad they called Shovey. After the foot race, we watched a game with a leather ball. The organizers marked out a one hundred yard by fifty yard area. There were two teams opposing one another and the object was to carry the ball over the hundred yard line as many times as they could in thirty minutes. The opposing team did their best to stop them. It was great fun, especially when one boy who they called Malcky McKewan ran about three hundred yards as he dodged from side to side and around in circles, ultimately going too far and diving over the wrong line, scoring nothing. Everyone laughed at his mistake and so did he. Next, it was time for the hundred yard dog race. The owners went to the finishing line while the handlers held the dogs at the start. We noticed that Joshua was one of the entries. The owners called and whistled and the dogs raced towards them. They were all level at the half way mark, including Joshua, until the dogs started chasing a squirrel that ran across the track. It was hilarious to watch the owners fall over one another as they tried desperately to catch them. The squirrel eventually ran up a tree and sat there, laughing. The king roared with laughter and said that he had not seen anything this funny in a long time. We watched the strong men next, as they threw round stones and tossed long poles. It was a very tense finish in the final but a Galashiels lad named Davey Johnson won. This completed a lovely and entertaining afternoon. We thanked King Logan for his hospitality and promised to come back one day soon.

It was sad to say goodbye to bonnie Scotland that night as we flew away back to Wales.

It began to pour down with rain not long after. This made us lose our way, causing us to end up over a tiny village called Llangwm. We flew into a wood behind a small church and slept there for the night.

When I awoke, the rain had stopped and the sun had been up for at least an hour. Tianaju was up already and had breakfast made.

"Good morning," she said to me.

"Good morning, early fairy. It looks as if it's going to be a lovely day today," I remarked.

She was cooking something that smelled just wonderful so I enquired, "What are you making?"

She answered, "It's pancakes. I got the flour, eggs, honey and milk from the farm next to the church. Come and try them, they are lovely."

She was absolutely right; they were lovely, especially when she covered them with the delicious honey. When we had finished, she washed up and put everything away in the coach. To my surprise, she emerged from the coach dressed head to toe in red.

"Wow, where are you going dressed like that?" I asked.

"Nowhere special. I thought I'd put something nice on for a change. After all, it is our last day.

Would you like to take a look at the little church before we set off home?"

I replied, "Yes, alright. It looks very interesting."

Once inside, we found that it was lovely and very peaceful as we sat there in silence. I was curious now and began thinking to myself, "What is it that she's going to tell me today? I hope it's not about Ohibronoeler or another catastrophe."

She nudged me and whispered, "Come on let's go for a walk."

We came out from the church and took a walk up the narrow country road. The farmers had recently collected their last load of hay so the fields were all clear. The hedgerows were entwined with honeysuckle and brambles and the ditches were full of prickly thistles. There were two different types of thistles; there were the ordinary prickly ones that grew in the ditch and the lovely, soft purple ones without prickles that grew along the grass verge. We walked for a while but Tianaju seemed to be far away, thinking. She was happy, but it was unusual for her to be so quiet. It was a lovely day so I just walked at her side and left her to her thoughts. We came to a style and she sat down on the step.

I can't even tell you how lovely she looked, sitting there with honeysuckle at each side of her and soft purple thistles at her feet. She was looking at me with her beautiful green eyes as if she was about to say something, but hesitated.

She looked so beautiful that suddenly, I plucked up some courage and picked one of the lovely soft thistles, knelt down on my knee, and handed it to her saying, "Tianaju will you marry me?"

As I knelt there, her lovely eyes began to fill with tears as she asked me, "Are you serious, Welusa?"

Then I thought to myself, "Oh no! What have I said? How can I marry a fairy? I'm so stupid and now I have made her cry. Oh! What am I going to do now? What will I say?"

I quickly stood up and said, "Oh please forgive me Tianaju. I am so sorry that I made you cry. I don't know what came over me. I was only joking, that's all. I know that you will never get married."

She stood up and said her favorite two words, "Oh you!" Then she pushed me into the ditch, which was full of prickly thistles. As I climbed out, she pushed me back in again saying, "I will." She hesitated, and then added, "I am getting married."

I was stunned after hearing her tell me this. I led there for a while before climbing out saying, "What! You are really getting married? Why didn't you tell me?" I thought you never wanted to get married."

She replied, "Yes I do. It's been thirty-five years since I found the meaning to my name and the same length of time since I decided not to marry, but I have fallen in love…."

I interrupted her and said "It's okay, it's okay, there is no need for you to say any more, I understand. It was just a surprise to me, that's all. I am very pleased for you."

I looked at her smiling face then added, "You can keep the thistle, it might bring you luck. Oh, by the way, give me a hand to pull the rest of these prickly ones out of my pants? They are killing me."

This made her laugh, but as we walked back to the coach, it was my turn to be in a dream now.

I just couldn't believe what she had told me. It was like losing the only thing I ever cared about.

I was curious now, so I said to her, "You told me that you will live until the end of time and never grow old."

She said, "Yes, that's true."

"Well, what about your husband?" I asked.

She replied, "I was told that if I decide to marry, my husband will also live until the end of time."

She then slipped her arm in mine and said, "I have to go back to Fairyland tonight for a week to talk with my father, but I will be back to take you once again to Vanbolena. The whole of Fairyland is waiting just for you. You will spend a week with me and my family who are all waiting to see you again, especially my Mother and Father."

Later, we carried on into the tiny village of Usk and stayed there for the rest of the afternoon. In the evening she told me, "I have to go now but I will be knocking on your door next Sunday evening."

She kissed me on the cheek, pointed her wand towards the coach, and in a puff of magic it vanished along with her.

I collected Lianga and set off through the town of Usk. We took our time walking up the valley roads, through Llanover village, up past old Abe's farm, down the mountain road, passing by the chapel on the corner, and finally on to my home about a mile away in Afon Llwyd.

My mother and father were happy to see me again but were disappointed when I told them that I was off again next week. I showed my mother the lovely suit of clothes that I had worn in Hawick.

She loved them and asked, "These must have cost you a fortune. How could you ever afford them?"

I answered, "Well, it's all to do with the book I wrote. Someone rich in Scotland loved it and gave me the suit of clothes as a present."

She put the suit away in my cupboard, chuckled and said, "I'll have to watch your father or he'll be after it to wear down to the tavern, showing off."

My father just laughed and assured her saying, "I'm not a Scotsman. Besides, the suit would never fit me."

During that week, I did some more work on my book and in the evenings I went out with my mates. When Sunday evening came, there was a knock on my door. I quickly answered it and to my delight, it was my beaming Tianaju, dressed in the same riding clothes.

"Well, here I am as I promised," she reminded me.

I helped her off with her cape and said, "Come on in, my mother and father are expecting you."

She then asked, "Can you sign and date one of my life story books and bring it with you when we leave?"

My parents welcomed her into our home again and we sat down and chatted over tea and my mother's homemade Welsh cakes. Later, I left the three of them happily chatting away while I went upstairs to fetch the book she wanted. We stayed for another hour before saying goodbye once again to my parents.

My mother said, "Oh well, It was nice to see you again for five minutes Juanita. Take care, the both of you."

They waved as we walked away up the Keepers Hill to collect Lianga. When we got to the top I looked across towards the Dragon's Pond and said, "I wonder what he is doing now."

Tianaju held my hand and said, "Don't worry; we are safe now, thanks to you."

She looked down at herself and said, "Now to get rid of these old riding clothes."

With a sprinkle of magic from her wand, she was wearing a lovely purple dress with a red sash around her waist, and red shoes with purple buckles. Then to my surprise her flickering wings appeared once again behind her.

I sighed, gently shook my head and said, "You look absolutely lovely."

You can just imagine how I felt that night, knowing that one day she would be lost to me forever. I knew that day would soon be here and I wasn't looking forward to it in the least. Especially after I heard her say, "I hope I will never have to wear those riding clothes ever again."

Then, with another wave, the lovely shiny coach appeared with Lianga once again coupled up to it.

I noticed now that her wand was back to normal size again. I was about to get another surprise. She told me to get my book ready because we were off to Kansas in America to deliver it to the little blind girl.

I was excited and said "America! Okay let's go."

She explained to me, "We will have to wait until three in the morning because Kansas is five hours behind us"

We sat in the coach and she began to tell me about some of the places she had visited throughout the world. Listening to her fascinating stories made the time pass really quickly. She smiled when she finished, looked up at the moon and said,

"Its three o'clock now, come on, let's go to Kansas."

We climbed aboard the coach and off we went, heading across the Atlantic Ocean to America. It couldn't have taken us long to get there, because I cannot remember a thing about it until we set down just outside a farm house.

Tianaju pointed to an upstairs window, "That's her room, have you signed the book?" she asked.

"Yes I have. Here it is," I replied.

She took the book and said, "Thank you I won't be long. Don't fly away, will you?"

I replied, "Ha ha. Well I might."

She took the book and flew through the unopened window. It was only a matter of minutes before I heard the excited girl squeal with delight. It made me feel so happy that my eyes began to fill up with emotion.

Tianaju came back through the window beaming her lovely smile saying, "Well that's one happy little girl."

She flew up beside me and put her hand on my knee and said, "Come on, let's go home."

In a flash, we were heading for the clear white half moon that was surrounded by twinkling, happy looking stars. As I looked down, even the moonbeams seemed to be dancing with joy as we flew. After we flashed through the coloured bubble and into Fairyland, I could hear cheering.

"It's you they are cheering for," said the happy queen.

I couldn't see anyone but it was an incredible sound that seemed to be all around us. As we landed at the gateway to the city, all the cheering fairies appeared in their millions. They all formed an archway, which led all the way up to the gates of Vanbolena Castle.

Nabalion was there to greet us at the City gates. He bowed his head as his queen stepped down from the coach.

"Welcome, your majesty, and to you, Welusa," he said in his deep voice.

I jumped down from the coach and joined her. As I did so, she waved her wand and the lovely coach vanished.

"Come, Welusa, through the only fairy arch in the history of Fairyland. They are all waiting to honour you."

She flew up onto Nabalion as I mounted my hero Lianga. We made our way through the most beautiful archway I had ever seen. The road ahead of us was lit up and strewn with yellow rose petals. Above us, the excited fairies, dressed in sparkling lilac and yellow, were gently floating down the petals. The sound of them cheering in harmony simply overwhelmed me. They were praising us saying, "Praise to Tianaju, the Emerald Queen of Children and Welusa the saviour of the moon."

I just couldn't believe that they were calling me that. Tianaju looked across and pointed at me, smiling as if to say. "Yes that's you."

All through the city and outside every house and shop, flags were flying. One pretty little fairy flew up and kissed me on the cheek saying, "Thank you."

Tianaju shouted over, "That's Simone, our tooth fairy."

I shouted back, "She's lovely, isn't she?"

The magnificent pure white Nabalion swayed his head from side to side as he proudly carried his beautiful queen through the city.

Lianga was also walking with a spring in his step so I leaned over and whispered in his ear,

"I am so proud of you. I couldn't have achieved anything without you."

He swished his tail and replied, "This is the proudest moment of my life."

The peal of the three bells of Vanbolena Cathedral could be heard in the distance. The nearer we got the louder and more glorious they sounded. Lianga was absolutely enjoying himself, especially when another little fairy flew over and kissed him on his nose. After that it was a free for all, as more and more fairies came in smothering both of us with kisses all the way up to the castle gates. Waiting at the gates were twelve guards with Prince Aiden, their captain. Tianaju told me that they were her own guards of honour. They marched with six on each side of us with Prince Aiden marching in front. When we reached the castle doors, Prince Aiden roared out a command and the great wooden doors opened. We entered the castle, walked into the great hall and there to greet us was King Drahol and Queen Roaniler, her twin sister Princess Anoralee and her husband Prince Salown.

Tianaju hugged and kissed them all.

The king welcomed me once again into their home, "Welcome, Welusa. We are really proud of you and will be forever grateful. You were brave and courageous beyond the verge of impossibility. We will be forever in your debt. Your name will be etched on the Great Bell of Wonder that hangs above the historic Balance Arch. Each time it rings, the whole of Fairyland will be reminded of you and how you saved the moon from darkness."

I thanked the king saying, "Thank you great king. I am deeply honoured to have my name on such a sacred bell. As far as you and Fairyland being in debt to me, I disagree. Your lovely daughter gave me the privileged position of being able to enter your enchanting kingdom. I was then given the honour of meeting you, your family and all your delightful fairies. So when she asked me for my help, I considered it to be another great honour. I was also given the ability to speak to Nabalion, Lianga and all the other animals. I was even able to see the mighty winds and the magic moonbeams. It was wondrous. Finally, I was able to spend time with your beautiful daughter and although the mission was sometimes dangerous, I enjoyed every minute of it.

It may seem strange to you, but we spent most of our time laughing. So, dear king, I want you and Fairyland to know that you owe me nothing. This, I must insist."

He was stunned for a while then tapped me on my arm and said, "You are a good man Welusa. You must be tired now?"

He clapped his hands and the lovely fairy maid, Laura, came in and curtsied. The king looked at me and said, "Laura will be your personal maid for as long as you stay. She will take you to your room. So, sleep well Welusa."

I followed Laura to the same fabulous room I was given before. I was so tired that I collapsed on the lovely, soft bed and fell sound asleep.

When I awoke it was midday and I found to my delight that I was still on the bed and not on the floor. Laid out on a chair beside my bed was a suit of clothes for me. It was a red and green, full welsh tartan outfit with a kilt. I had only ever worn such a grand suit of clothes once before and that was at the masked ball in Hawick. It was only the rich that could afford such a lovely outfit. There was also a steaming hot bath drawn across the room.

"Wow, that looks great," I said to myself. "I'm off straight in there now."

After the lovely bath, I felt like a new man again especially with my brand new clothes on.

Laura who was in the process of putting my old clothes away said, "You look fabulous Welusa. Just like a Welsh Prince."

"Well I'm not sure about that, but thank you anyway," I replied.

In fact I looked so grand that I was embarrassed to join the royal family for lunch. I didn't know where to look as they all complimented me.

After lunch Tianaju informed me, "In honour of you, we are having a royal banquet this evening. It will be held in the castle grounds. All the royals from Fairyland will be there and a thousand fairies from our city of Vanbolena."

I asked her, "What is a royal banquet?"

She answered, "A royal banquet is where folk are invited to a palace by a king or queen. A feast of different varieties of food will be provided. The banquet will also give anyone that wishes, an opportunity to share their opinions or to show their appreciations in a speech. So, my father has invited the royals and a thousand fairies to honour you."

She could see that I was looking very worried, so she took hold of my arm and said, "Don't worry, you don't have to say anything. The speeches will not be too long, but there might be a lot of thankful fairies kissing you later on."

"Well, I better not eat any onions then," I joked.

Then, to my dismay, she told me that she had to meet someone and wouldn't be back until later that afternoon.

"That's okay," I said. "Will it be alright with everyone, if I take Lianga and walk around the city until the banquet begins?"

She replied, "Yes, certainly. You are free to go wherever you wish."

So that is what I did and it turned out to be one of the nicest days I had ever experienced. I walked through the city and Lianga walked behind me. As I walked through I was stopped by lovely lady fairies who welcomed me into their homes. It was fortunate for me that fairies are of human size but no taller than five feet three otherwise I would not have been able to get through their doors. Their homes were absolutely lovely. If I were to tell you that everything in their beautiful homes was made from oak, silk, velvet, coloured glass, silver and gold, together with a touch of sparkling fairy magic, it might give you a good idea of how fabulous they were. In fact, if you close your eyes and imagine Fairyland, it will be exactly as you want it to be, because the beauty of Fairyland is absolutely indescribable.

In each one of these splendid homes I was offered, as is the fairy custom, a thimble of fairy juice. This juice is made from a sweet flower called Zelenia, which only grows on the nights when the moon is full and it tastes just wonderful. One of my highlights that day was when I was welcomed into a lovely little cottage that belonged to two very pretty fairy sisters. Their names were May and Mary. They excitedly showed me around their lovely home called Lilac Cottage. It was the quaintest little cottage that I have ever seen. After they finished showing me around, we enjoyed some of their lovely fairy cakes. Before I left, I sat down on the couch to have a chat and they both squashed in beside me. So, as I was squashed in the middle, both of them, but especially Mary, started giggling.

May informed me, "Mary is very mischievous."

Mary exclaimed, "No I am not!" Then she kissed me on my cheek.

May then said, "Oh Mary." Then, kissed me on the other cheek.

We had a good old chat and laughed for a while. Then, after about three or four attempts to leave, they finally let me up. All I can say is, when I was ready to go, it was a little difficult trying to get out of their door with Mary and May hanging on to each of my arms.

All the fairies I visited were coming to the banquet anyway, so I told them that I would see them all again later.

I left them, mounted Lianga and we made our way to nearly the top of a cold mountain they call The Coity. It was chilly but lovely, sitting there looking down at the beautiful city. Lianga wandered off and I sat there, talking to myself, "Mmm it's nice and peaceful here. I wonder who it is Tianaju has gone to see."

All the fairies I visited were very excited about her wedding. The exciting wedding was to be at one minute past midnight, Sunday the twenty eighth of July next year. They told me that her wedding will be the most romantic wedding that has ever been. When I asked them why, they told me it was because she will be married on the only day the new moon has ever began at midnight.

I shook my head and said out loud, "It was stupid of me that day when I asked her to marry me. What was I thinking of?"

I knew that during our time together I fell in love with her, but to ask her to marry me was the dumbest thing I have ever said in my life.

I settled down, then, once again muttered to myself, "I just hope I don't get an invite to the wedding, because I will never be able to watch it. Anyway, I wish her well because she deserves it."

In the distance, I heard the tower clock strike five so I thought we had better make our way back to the castle. When we arrived at the castle, there were many fairy maids and butlers busy with the preparations. Lianga went off to his stable and I went up to my room. I found another bath waiting there for me. So, once again I dove in and came out refreshed.

I felt very nervous later, as Laura knocked on my door asking, "Are you ready Welusa? They are all waiting for you."

I opened the door and said, "Yes, I am. Come on, let's go down."

Tianaju was waiting at the entrance to the hall. She looked absolutely stunning as she stood there smiling. She was wearing a three quarter length, emerald green, velvet dress edged with pearls. Her hair was swept up into an elegant bun, held in place by a silver band of green sparkling butterflies. Around her back and looped over her arms but not her shoulders, was a white shawl edged once again with pearls. As she walked towards me I could see that she was wearing an emerald on a gold chain around her neck. Although the colour of her lovely emerald necklace and shiny green dress was incredible, her beautiful eyes outshone them both. I was so entranced with her that I didn't hear a word she was saying, until she held both my hands, shaking them and saying, "Come on, Welusa. They are waiting."

As we walked into the great hall we were greeted by loud applause. After the applause died down, Tianaju introduced me to all the royal families and guests.

With the introductions over, we all went outside, as the banquet was to be held in the castle grounds. As we were about to take our seats at the banquet table, I mentioned to Tianaju, "You haven't introduced me to your husband to be yet. Where is he? Will he be arriving later on?"

She answered, "This is your week in Fairyland so it's only right that we enjoy it together."

I was just about to tell her, "That's fine with me," when the trumpets sounded. They were announcing the arrival of King Drahol and Queen Roaniler.

The king wore a magnificent gold-coloured suit and the queen was dressed in lilac with a white shawl around her shoulders. Her lovely dress looked as if it was made from silk as it rippled and changed colour as she walked.

The king told everyone to take their seats as the banquet was about to commence. He then struck a gong and immediately the waiters and waitresses came out, carrying the lovely food that had been prepared. They set it on the tables and we all began to enjoy it. The food was the best that I had ever tasted. I sat back in my chair and thought that I might never be able to move again.

It was at that point that the king rose and called for order, as he was about to make a speech. He was the first of many royals that honoured me that evening. It was embarrassing sitting there listening to them treating me like a great warrior, when all I had done really, was enjoy every bit of the mission I was given. Tianaju squeezed my hand and smiled at me.

After the last speech, I thought it only right that I thanked them. So I did, and assured them, just as I assured King Drahol, that they were in no way in debt to me. I told them that I loved every minute of my mission and if they ever needed help again, I would be the first to volunteer.

After saying that, Tianaju gently kicked me. As I looked at her, she squinted and nodded her head.

So I added, "Oh yes! That is, just as long as Tianaju comes too."

"That's better," she said.

Everyone laughed, saying, "She wouldn't want it any other way."

My embarrassment left me after that and I felt great. I really did appreciate how grateful they were to me. So I picked up a glass of orangeade and said, "I would like to make a toast to Fairyland, may it continue reigning with love forever."

They all stood up with their glasses saying,

"To Fairyland, forever more."

Tianaju looked at me with watery eyes and said, "Thank you that was a lovely thing to say."

King Drahol clapped his hands and said, "It's time for dancing. Everyone enjoy yourselves the night is young."

The busy servants cleared all the tables and workers set up the stage for the band. The castle grounds were now full of chatting fairies as we waited for the workers to finish. Tianaju took me up to the balcony overlooking the grounds. When the band arrived and the thousand fairies began to dance, it looked simply wonderful. It was a sight that I will never forget. They were so excited. I could never imagine anyone being as happy as they were that evening. Both Tianaju and I joined them later and that was when I must have had the thousands of kisses that she warned me about. Every one of those fairies was so pretty, I just could not believe I was being kissed by so many of them. If you were to ask me if I enjoyed it I would say, "What do you think?"

Princess Stacey and the lovely tooth fairy Simone were the stars of the night as they both danced the Diamond Tooth Ballet. They were simply wonderful.

After that, Tianaju suggested, "Shall we show everyone how to dance the Scottish Reel?"

I replied, "Okay, that should be fun. Come on then! Let's teach them."

It didn't take long before everyone knew all the steps. King Drahol fell in love with the new dance and by magic, conjured up some Scottish bagpipes and fiddles for the band to play. At first, it was very funny to watch the fairies dance and fall over one another. Once they mastered it though, the atmosphere in the castle grounds was quite amazing, especially as we were now dancing the reel to traditional Scottish music. It was tremendous fun as we changed partners time and time again. We changed so many times that I didn't know where I was by the end of it. Eventually, I finished up opposite the smiling Tianaju once more and was thankful for it. We danced quite a few more reels and followed by some more unusual fairy dances.

Then, Tianaju decided to show her father another Scottish dance that she had learned. The king was happy for her to show him this new dance because he was glad to have a rest. She went back into the castle and came out wearing the lovely Scottish outfit she wore in Hawick. She took to the stage, had a word with the band and gave a marvelous display of a Scottish jig. All of bonnie Scotland would have been proud of her. She was, and looked, simply amazing. Soon, every other fairy that was watching wanted to have a go. Never in the history of highland dancing have so many danced the jig at the same time. It was hilarious. I have never heard such laughter in my life. Even the king and queen joined in and were soon doubled over in stitches. This went on until no one could dance anymore from laughing. Then, to my dismay, they all pointed at me and chanted that it was my turn to do a solo jig. So, with great reluctance, I had to oblige and climbed up onto the stage. I started off great and was doing really well until I got a little bit carried away and to a roar of laughter fell backwards off the end of the stage.

I jumped back up, gave a bow and said, "How is that for an ending?"

After a night of laughter and energetic dancing it was a relief to hear the band start to play a soft slow waltz which was the last dance of the night. I had never danced the waltz with Tianaju before, so to hold my arm around her small waist that night was so wonderful, I didn't want it to end. Unfortunately, it did end, but it was lovely while it lasted.

To close out the evenings events there was a dazzling display of coloured magic from every fairy's wand shooting and swirling up into the night sky. It lasted until the king's trumpeters sounded the end of a glorious night. Everyone thanked the king and queen for a lovely time and went home happily chatting away. I, too, thanked them for a lovely time and wished them both good night.

Tianaju and I wished each other the same and I went to my room extremely happy. I washed, changed into my nightshirt, climbed into a nice, soft, warm bed and fell sound asleep watching the twinkling stars through an open window.

If I was happy after that first night, you can imagine how I felt after an entire week of fun and games. It felt like every fairy in the land wanted to please me. I had never been so happy in my life.

On my last day there, Tianaju and I had a picnic on the lush green grass beside Vanbolena Lake. We spent the afternoon reminiscing about our adventures. We shuddered, as we remembered the misery and torment that Ohibronoeler and the hostile people had subjected us to. But, the bad times were soon forgotten as we laughed at the happy and funny moments that came to mind. There were quite a few. Though, I did feel a little sorry for Ohibronoeler, stuck in the pond, never to get out. Tianaju assured me that he could never be trusted. He would always have plenty of food and that he could breathe under water like a fish. It was the best place for him. We also wondered just what the winds were doing now. Were they still all friends and talking about their finest battle with Ohibronoeler? It was a very ferocious battle, which we were sure they had exaggerated even more by now! Or have they fallen out again? We pictured them arguing about who played the greatest part in the defeat of the dragon. We were sure that Howler and his father would be trying to claim this honour, as it was Howler that lifted me up to toss that lovely lock of Tianaju's hair. This we will never know, for I had no intensions of ever going back to find out.

I took a few deep breaths before I said to Tianaju, "Well, I had better be going back to Wales tonight and hopefully back to work next week. I suppose all of Fairyland will be very busy from now on, preparing for your wedding. They are all very excited about it."

She answered, "Yes you are right. There is a lot to do before the wedding, but I am sure a little bit of magic will help."

We walked back through the city only to be greeted by a load of fairies practicing the Scottish jig. They looked so cute and lovely that I felt sad knowing that I was going to miss them all and that I might never see them again.

As we walked through the castle gates I asked her, "After you are married will you still visit the children to tell them your life story?"

She replied, "Yes, I will, and I will do so until the end of time. Every month for three nights when the moon is full I will visit as many children as I can throughout your world. This I have promised."

After our evening meal, as we all sat in the living room, the king also made a promise to me saying, "Welusa, I promise you that before I die Tianaju will reveal to you a secret. It will be something wonderful that will make you happy for the rest of your life."

I replied, "Thank you, great king. I will look forward to receiving it, but hopefully you will live for many years after."

He laughed and said, "So do I."

I went on to sadly say, "I will never forget the kindness that you, your family and your lovely fairies have shown me during the time I have spent in your wonderful land. I will miss you all."

I soon cheered up later on as I said to myself, "Well Welusa, just think, if you had never met the beautiful queen you would never have had the best time of your life. So now, you will always have lovely memories to tell your children one day."

In the evening, Tianaju and I went to the top of the castle. It was very emotional for me as I looked out at the amazing city for the last time.

While we were talking I asked Tianaju, "Where are you going to live after you are married?"

She pointed to a large cloud then answered, "We are going to live in Juanita Castle, over there on Blorenge Hill. It is a wedding gift from my Father and Mother. They have secretly hidden it with that silver cloud until we are married."

Then the moment I had been dreading arrived. My heart sunk as she turned to me because I knew she was going to invite me to the wedding saying, "Welusa, will you…"

I stopped her at that point and said, "I uh I mean uh."

"You mean what!" she asked, as I walked away.

I said, "I uh I forgot what I was going to say again."

"Oh! Trust you." she said.

I scratched my head then said, "Wait a minute." Then thought, "If I tell her that it will be hard for me to watch the one I love marry someone else, it will probably upset her. So I had better think of something quickly."

I paced around a little then said, to myself, "Right, that's it. I know what to say."

I looked at her and my heart sunk even more, because her lovely face turned to anguish as she waited for me to speak. So with my fingers crossed behind my back, I said, "Much as I would love to come to the wedding, it will not be possible. On my return home I'll have to beg for my job back. With your wedding in July, the same time as harvesting, it will be very difficult for me to ask for time off. So, I'm sure you can appreciate how awkward it will be for me to attend the wedding. But, I promise that I will be there in spirit, sending you all my love as the Town Crier calls midnight."

She answered sympathetically, "I understand."

So she was okay with my excuse and I was happy that she didn't persist.

"Well, I suppose I had better get ready for the ride back home then. Is Nabalion taking me?"

She answered, "Nabalion and I are taking you."

I thought, "That's the last thing I want." So I said, "I would rather say goodbye to you here than say goodbye to you in Wales."

She replied, "Alright, if you would rather it be that way, I understand."

We made our way down the beautiful winding stone stairway, picked up my bag then headed for the great hall where I would say goodbye to everyone. As I walked into the hall, they were all smiling.

I looked at them and thought, "Why am I feeling so sad while everyone looks so happy? I must pull myself together and be like them."

The king informed me saying, "You will always be able to talk with the animals, trees and the winds. So if there is anything else I can do for you, you can tell Simone, our tooth fairy. She will be calling in on you from time to time."

I didn't feel too bad saying goodbye after that, except when I had to say goodbye to the beautiful Emerald Queen of Children.

That was really tough and emotional for me, but by then I had accepted the fact that I was just a lovesick fool who should have known better than to fall in love with her. She belonged in Fairyland and I belonged in my own world. To ever think of marrying such a beautiful fairy was ridiculous. That kind of thing only happens in dreams.

It was Lianga and not Nabalion that was waiting for me in the court yard that night.

Tianaju had surprised me by saying, "As a token of my appreciation for all that you did for me and Fairyland, Lianga is yours now for as long as you wish."

"Wow! Thank you very much," I said excitedly.

The lovely queen once again thanked me for everything and wished me well.

I held her hands and looked at her beautiful face, gazed into her watery eyes and said, "I love ... I loved every moment that we spent together. I'll never forget you."

I put my arms around her and we hugged. The scent of her frankincense and myrrh perfume made my heart sink again, but I was determined to be strong. So we said good bye and as I mounted Lianga she called out to me, "Welusa, haven't you forgotten something?"

I replied, "I don't think so. What is it?"

She answered, "Aren't you going to kiss me good bye?"

I looked at her and thought, "One kiss from her and I'll never go home."

So I smiled and said, "Well I might." Then I added as we rose into the air, "In my dreams."

She shook her finger at me and said, "Oh you, you pest. I'll get you for that. Maybe I won't let you kiss me in your dreams."

She then beamed her lovely smile, blew me a kiss and waved with both hands.

I said to myself as I waved back and smiled, "Phew I nearly told her."

As we passed over the city all the pretty fairies were waving and blowing kisses at me so I blew a few back.

It didn't take us long to reach the bubble and as we flew through it, I sighed as I whispered, "Good bye Fairyland."

We landed once again beside the Keepers Pond and I thanked Lianga for everything. He gave me a gentle nudge with his nose and said, "It's okay Welusa, I enjoyed the adventure. It was great. What are you going to do now?"

I answered, "Oh, I'll try to get work at the farm again and later, hopefully finish the story of our incredible adventure. Maybe one day, if the book sells, I will have my own farm. In the meantime you are free to do as you wish. So please take care of yourself my dear friend."

He replied, "I will, Welusa, but I am not going anywhere. You and I are a team now so if you want me, all you have to do is whistle. In case you've forgotten, I can fly now so I will be with you in a jiffy."

I patted him on his neck and said, "Well, I guess that makes you my partner. So I'll see you when I see you then, O bird horse."

He laughed then trotted away saying, "Yeah, see you later, O Warrior."

I walked down the hill to my home and threw a tiny stone at my parent's bedroom window. This woke my mother up and she quickly came down to let me in.

"Hello Mam I'm back to stay now, my work is finished and I am all worn out."

"Go on in and give that fire a poke, you look so pale. I'll make you a nice mug of hot milk to warm you up," she said as she took my jacket from me.

I looked at her and said to myself, "If ever I find a wife, I hope she is just as lovely as her."

She came in with the milk and said, "There now, that will warm you up. I'll go and make your bed now. You can tell me everything in the morning. Good night, son."

It was difficult to get to sleep that night from thinking. When I did eventually fall asleep, my mother told me that she had to call me five or six times before I woke up.

After breakfast she remarked, "I have never seen you so tired before, Welusa. What on earth have you been doing? Where have you been? Who gave you that beautiful Welsh tartan suit this time?"

I stood up and replied, "Well Mam, firstly, as you know, I have been traveling all around the country delivering messages for Juanita. Secondly, I enjoyed every moment I spent delivering them. It was the best job I could have ever wished for. Thirdly, Juanita gave me the suit of clothes as a present. Last of all I uh, umm I, I loved riding the horse."

"Ah don't give me that, Welusa. Loved riding the horse indeed! You fell in love with that pretty girl, didn't you? Where is she? Are you going to see her again?" asked my concerned mother.

I twisted my answer saying, "Mam! Don't be silly, she was just my boss, that's all. She doesn't love me; in fact, she's getting married next July. As for seeing her again, maybe I will, if she wants me to work for her again."

"Ah you are hiding something from me Welusa. But that's you, I suppose. You always did."

I gave her a kiss on the cheek and said, "But I love you though, don't I Mam? Now, I'm off to see Peter about getting my job back. Ta ra Mam, see you later."

I called up to the farm and Peter was happy to see me, "Nice to see you again, Welusa. Come in. How are you getting on in your new job?" he asked.

He knew I was traveling around the country delivering messages.

So I told him, "For months now I have done quite a lot of running around and finally ran out of wind."

He laughed and said, "Well I suppose that means your work has come to an end then? So if you want your old job back, Gwydion will be pleased to see you again. You can start on Monday if you'd like."

I thanked him and said, "I'll see you Monday then."

As I walked down to the town, I just couldn't help wondering what Gwydion would say when he finds out that I can talk to him. "That should be fun," I said out loud.

My mother was out when I arrived home in the afternoon. Mostly every day she helps her sister Liza, who lives in Engine Row, clean the Church School that's at the bottom of the town. So I went to my room and continued working on my book.

I was glad that I made notes of almost every day that we spent on our travels. I could remember the whole experience, but having those notes made it easier for me.

In the evening I sat in the living room talking with my parents. My father told me that there was a lot of gossip going around. A dragon had been seen in the pond next to the Keepers Pond.

He asked me what I thought about it. I informed him, "Folk are always saying that there are some kind of strange creatures in their lakes and forests all the time. When I was in Scotland I was told that there was a creature in one of their lakes too. They called him the Loch Ness monster. The Scots say it's just a fairy tale."

My father picked up the clock and said, "Yes, someone is just messing around. I'll just wind up this old clock and then I'm off to bed." He then joked, "With my old dragon."

My mother laughed as she followed him up the stairs and said, "Dragon eh, well watch I don't bite you then, old man."

We said good night and I blew out the lamp and went to bed behind them.

The following day, which was Saturday, I went down town to pick up some ink and found that almost everyone there was talking about the dragon.

Brenhilda Stokes asked me, "Are you going up to the Dragon's Pond, Welusa?

I pretended that I knew nothing, so I answered, "What dragon's pond?"

She answered, "The one next to the Keepers Pond. People say there's a dragon in there."

So I said, "Well, I might take a look later."

I went home, put my ink away, and then took a walk up to the dragon's pond. When I arrived at the pond, there were quite a lot of people peering into it. I knew Ohibronoeler would be lying on the bottom, out of sight, waiting for them to go away. I was just about to go back home when Cindy came up to me and asked, "Have you seen the dragon today, Welusa?"

I replied, "No, I haven't seen him today, have you?"

She answered, "Yes, I think I saw his nose this morning. Where do you think he came from Welusa?"

All I could think of was, "Oh he probably came in with the wind."

"Oh yes, it was windy a few weeks ago wasn't it, Welusa?"

"Yes, you are right Cindy, it was very windy. We can safely say, he came in with the wind. Come on, I'll take you down if you are going?"

She replied, "No, I'll stay here. He just might pop up again."

"Okay, I am off then, Cindy."

"Will I see you tomorrow evening for the walk down Cwmavon road, Welusa?"

"Yes, Cindy, if it's fine."

As I headed back down to work on my book I said to myself, "Won't they all be surprised if they ever get to read it."

I went home and straight upstairs to carry on with my writing.

My mother shouted up to me, "Are you still writing that silly old book?"

I shouted back down, "No, I'm writing a good one." I laughed to myself and added, "If you call my book silly again I'll write you in as a monkey."

She just laughed and shouted back, "I thought your dad said I was a dragon?"

She was always joking around. She caught me once on April Fool's day when she called upstairs one morning for school, telling me I was late. I rushed downstairs, gobbled my breakfast, kissed her goodbye, and ran out the door as far as the gate. On the gate was a note saying, "April Fool, it's Saturday."

It was raining Sunday evening so no one went out for a walk. Cindy was disappointed because she loved the trips down Cwmavon road. Every night for two more weeks I stayed in my room trying to finish the story. It was coming along very well and I was pleased with it. Each night my lovely mother would bring me up a sandwich and a mug of hot milk. I stayed up until three o'clock one Sunday morning and by then, my book was nearly finished. I was now at the point where I had to recall the last week that I spent with Tianaju in Vanbolena.

Although I enjoyed every minute of my time there, I was finding it extremely hard to put the events down on paper. I knew that once I wrote the last chapter it would be the end of my time with the beautiful Emerald Queen of Children. Sadness overwhelmed me and I kept putting it off time after time because I couldn't bear the thought of losing her again.

It was the beginning of December and all the trees were bare. Winter was upon us now but the weather was fine. So, I decided to give my writing a rest. On Sunday evening I joined some of the lads and lassies for the traditional evening stroll down Cwmavon road. It was dark but we were lucky because the moon was out, giving us a nice light. It didn't matter anyway because the darker it was, the more fun it was.

Cindy was happy to see me and called out, "Welusa I've missed you. Come on, let's go."

I gently twisted her wheelchair around and said, "Okay then, get on your marks."

I then ran pushing the laughing Cindy for about one hundred yards down the road.

"That was great Welusa," she said as I stopped.

"Puweee the last time I did that I was twelve months younger," I told her.

It was great to get away from the story for a change. Although it was winter it was an unusually warm evening. We all enjoyed ourselves laughing and joking with one another. On our way back, if the nights were dark, we used to tell ghost stories just to make the girls scream. The only girl that didn't scream was Cindy because she liked telling them herself.

When we returned from our walk we all stood around the old Halleluiah lamppost talking until about ten o'clock. We heard Cliff the Town Crier shouting out the hour so I said, "Well, that's me for the night I'm off home, maybe I'll see you tomorrow night."

Cindy only lived around the corner and had gone in earlier. As we all began to walk our different ways Victoria who was in the same school as me, but a small bit older, asked, "Will you walk me home Welusa?"

This took me by surprise so I replied, "Um, yes okay."

So as we walked up the town she reminisced about the time I used to tell her, and her friends, Tianaju's life story. She told me that she had bought my book and loved it.

I told her that I was writing another story and hopefully someone will publish it soon.

"That's good news Welusa. Is it going to be exciting?" she asked.

I replied, "Well if you liked the last one you should also like the next one."

We arrived at her home across the other side of town and I wished her good night outside her gate. As I walked away she asked me, "Aren't you going to kiss me Welusa?"

I turned around and thought, "I've heard that before."

My reply was something that I was extremely sorry about later on.

I told her, "I might. Next week"

She went in and slammed the door behind her.

I went home feeling terrible about upsetting her and couldn't get to sleep. I just couldn't believe what I had done to the lovely Victoria. I felt really ashamed of myself. It was the first thing that came into my mind. Instead of telling her I would love to, I once again did something stupid by upsetting another lovely girl.

I said to myself, "The only girl I ever kissed is my mother and that's only on the cheek. So I must apologise to her when I see her next."

I tossed and turned all night long until I heard my mother call me for work. All I can remember that day is going to work and coming home. The rest of the day I was in a dream, thinking about the lovely queen and Victoria.

There were now seven months before the wedding, so I decided to finish the story. I had already been in touch with the printers in Swansea and they told me to bring it in when it was finished. So my plan was to collect Lianga and take it in the following Saturday morning. It would take them a few weeks to print it, and probably a further two more, until the American Publishers in England receive it.

As usual, my mother brought up my supper and kissed me good night. I sat in my bedroom with two flickering candles for light, finishing writing about my last week in Fairyland. Putting it into words without being too upset was tough for me. I was so tired from the lack of sleep the night before it was hard for me to stay awake. Eventually, without knowing it, I slumped forward on to the table and fell fast asleep all night.

The next thing I knew was my mother shouting, "Welusa! What have you done? Oh, Welusa!"

She gave me such a fright that I jumped up saying, "What! What's the matter?"

All I could see was a startled black bird flying out through the open window. Then, to my absolute horror, I saw what my mother was shouting about. My manuscript was ruined. While I slept I must have knocked my full mug of milk on to it. The milk had soaked right through the manuscript leaving the whole thing an inky mess. My face and arms were exactly the same.

I was in despair now saying, "Oh no, this is terrible, all my work is ruined."

"Never mind son, you go and clean up I'll gather up your papers for you. Don't worry yourself. There's plenty of time, you'll just have to start again," my mother said sympathetically.

It took me all day until I came home from work before I could come to terms with my disaster. My father tried to encourage me by saying, "I remember when you were a little lad, just beginning to walk, no matter how many times you fell down you never cried you just got back up, had a rest and laughed as you fell back down again. So just have a rest for a while son, until you are ready to go again."

That helped a small bit so I said, "Thanks Dad. I think I will." Then I slowly walked up the stairs to bed.

I was so depressed with losing my story that all I did was to go to work, come back home and mope about the house. On Sunday it was a cold but a dry night so I went out for the Sunday evening walk. I was hoping to see Victoria to apologise to her, but I was disappointed when my pals told me she had moved away and was working somewhere up the valley.

I enjoyed Christmas with my parents and celebrated the New Year with my friends. I did not start writing again until mid-spring. So one evening in April, I picked up my pen and once more began to write. So if you ever read this book Victoria, I now apologize to you. I was just a young fool.

It was the beginning of July before I almost finished it. I had only a few pages left to write but once again I had to recall my last week in Fairyland with the beautiful Fairy Queen I fell in love with. Once more I couldn't bring myself to even think about it.

So I asked Cindy to check over what I had written so far. She corrected a few sentences and spelling mistakes otherwise she said it was great.

She then asked, "How do you think up these stories Welusa?"

I whispered to her, "Magic."

She laughed and said, "Hey if you ever see her again ask her to call into me one night?"

I replied, "Yes I will. I promise."

After that I put the manuscript safely away for a while.

I said to my father, "Nearly finished Dad. So I am just going to have a rest."

"Well done my son, I knew you could do it," he replied.

Another two weeks went by and there was just one more before the wedding. So I decided late on Saturday night to take a walk up Keepers Hill. The Dragon's Pond was, by now, a well-established source of fascination for the local population. The whole town was trying to get a glimpse of him. Fortunately for Ohibronoeler no one had ever caught sight of him. All they have ever seen is the occasional swirl in the water, which they said was a fish. Whether they believe in the dragon or not, no one only the brave has ever swum in the Dragons Pond since.

When I arrived at the top of the hill there was no one around. So as I had never visited his pond for months I walked over, picked up a stick, and sat on the bank beside it. It wasn't long before his head popped up.

He swam over towards me and said, "Welusa my old pal. Where have you been? How are you getting on? Oh what's the matter dear boy? You look so miserable sitting there. I told you that she'd leave you, didn't I? I haven't slept a wink from worrying about you. She uses her beauty to snare and manipulate us weak and vulnerable men. You were a fool to listen to her, Welusa. The life story she told you was LIES, LIES, LIES. Oh Welusa, Welusa my poor boy my heart goes out to you. You have to believe me when I tell you that I am the true King of Fairyland. I was well known to be kind and gentle to all my fairies. Then, I met Tianaju and she fell in love with me. Although I fought desperately against it, I too fell head over heels in love with her. We were to be married within a year of loving one another. I was helplessly in love with her now and she knew it. Once she knew that I was devoted to her she began beating me with bunches of nettles making me scratch and itch all day. I begged for mercy but she just laughed. This went on until she and her father rebelled against me and threw me out of my beloved Fairyland. I was so in love with my beautiful bride to be that I didn't lift a finger to prevent it. Oh sweet Welusa, you remind me of myself, kind, gentle and honest. Help me Welusa. Help me to get out of here and back to myself. Find the Sun Giant for me. He is the only one that can release me from this dark deep pond. When I am free I will give you riches you'll never believe. What do you say Welusa, will you help your innocent friend?"

I replied, "Well Ohibronoeler, you were right, she has left me and ran off with someone else. She was dreadful to me. All she ever gave me was a magic horse that can fly and take me anywhere. She also left me with this dreadful ability to talk with the animals and trees. I can even talk to you. So I'll tell you what I'll do. I'll make a deal with you."

He asked excitedly, "Yes! You'll find the Sun Giant for me?"

I answered, "If you promise me that you'll give the children a ride on your back from time to time."

I hesitated, threw my stick into the pond, and shouted "Fetch." Then I added, "I promise you that every weekend I'll throw you a few more. What do you think of that, Rover?"

He was raging now and spat water at me saying, "You will be sorry for that Welusa. You, you, are nothing but a dirty rotten sneak, a sniveling love sick farm boy. I hope you spend the rest of your miserable life shoveling in the cow shed. I hope you always stay as ugly. It's no wonder why she left you. She's probably weeping now, sick with shame."

I walked away as he began frothing at the mouth stuttering out, "You, you, you're a looser, a stinking looser, a good for nothing lazy no good son of a coal miner, I'll give you throw me a stick, I hate you. Why, I hate you so much I hope all your hair falls out. I hope you grow a wart on your nose, you, you old witch you. Come back here yah coward and fight? I'll give you a bigger nose than the one you've already got. I'll get you one day Welusa. That's the only promise you'll get from me. I won't be in here forever."

I shouted back, "Oh and by the way, if ever I do find the Sun Giant, I'll tell him that you are a bad naughty boy and if you are really lucky he might throw you a stick."

I went home and paced about the house. I just couldn't rest. I kept thinking about what Ohibronoeler had said. My mother noticed that there was something wrong with me so she asked,

"What's the matter son? It's that girl Juanita again isn't it? You love her, don't you? Oh dear, trust you to get involved with someone so beautiful. She is getting married Welusa, so please try to forget about her. You are talking in your sleep almost every single night. I am worried about you, son. I just want you to be happy, that's all. So please don't upset yourself over pretty Juanita. You are such a nice looking boy, why don't you take out one of the lovely girls from town? They all like you, especially Ella."

She patted me on my shoulder and said, "I'll make us a nice mug of warm milk and we'll all go to bed. It's supposed to be a nice day tomorrow."

I went to bed and led there still feeling as if I was lost. I could see the last half moon through my window and thought, "I wonder what she is doing now. My mother said try and forget her. How can I forget her, I dream about her nearly every night. I hope I don't dream of her again tonight. Funny thing though in all my dreams I have never kissed her."

The following afternoon after church while I was weeding our flower bed, my mother came out to me and asked, "Welusa, I have been thinking. Has Juanita invited you to her wedding? If she has, remember that there is only a week to go."

She took me by surprise so I answered without thinking, "No she hasn't."

"What!" She exclaimed. "Why, that's terrible. After all you did for her. You tramped all around the countryside, wearing yourself out, covered in scars and lost about a stone in weight. So you mean to tell me that she never invited you to the wedding?"

I quickly thought, "What have I said. Now she thinks Tianaju is not a very nice person."

I crossed my fingers and replied, "Ah I was only kidding Mam, just like you do. Of course she invited me. Someone is fetching me at about eight o'clock Saturday evening, because she is getting married at midnight."

She raised her eyebrows and asked, "Midnight!"

I replied, "Yes. She thinks it's lucky to get married at the beginning of a new moon. Especially being the only one that begins at midnight for maybe centuries to come."

She laughed and said, "Midnight! I have never heard the likes of it. You must be kidding me again Welusa?"

I replied, "Well, just you wait and see Mam. Because at eight o'clock Saturday evening I'll be wearing my Welsh tartan suit and off up the Keepers to meet my ride."

She turned around saying, "Well if that's the case I'll set your suit out ready for you on Saturday. I'm off in now to make the tea."

I said to myself, "Trust me. Now what am I going to do? I'll be wandering around the mountain all night. I'll just have to take my tent and hide it somewhere before Saturday."

It was a lovely evening so I joined my pals for the Sunday walk. As usual, we all took it in turns pushing Cindy but it was me she wanted to give her the hundred yard dash. We all had a great time telling jokes and stories on our way back. The Sunday night walk always made us feel good, but going to sleep that night still wasn't easy. I had accepted that life with a fairy was impossible. But every time I closed my eyes, I could see her lovely face and hear us talking and laughing together.

By the time Friday came around, I was so worn out from lack of sleep that I was too tired to go to work. My mother let me sleep until lunch time. I would have stayed asleep a lot longer if it wasn't for her waking me to tell me that she had a nice hot bath ready. The bath was nice and it made me feel clean and fresh again.

My Mother tidied up my shirt collar and said, "There now, Welusa. You look a lot better now. After lunch why don't you go for a nice walk? I have told Peter that you needed a rest. He understood because he had noticed that you were looking very tired lately."

Later that afternoon, I went for a walk and at the same time managed to sneak out my tent. I hid it up on top of the Keeper's Hill and hoped that it wouldn't rain. I was feeling okay now and realised that if I wanted to be happy I had better start getting on with my life.

I said to myself, "After all I've got the loveliest mother in the world, a caring father, the best friends I could ever wish for, so what more do I want. Come on it's a beautiful world lets go and enjoy it. I only wish that I hadn't told my mother I had an invite to the wedding though."

I went home and told my mother that I was off upstairs to finish my story. That's just what I did except for the last few lines. I thought if I waited until after her wedding it would be a nice way to end the story. My mother and father were happy that I had finished it.

"Well done son," said my Dad. "Let's hope you'll sleep better now tonight."

I did sleep well that night until I felt a gentle kiss on my cheek. I opened my eyes and saw that it was Simone the Tooth Fairy. I sat up and said, "Wow! What are you doing here?"

"Good morning, Welusa. Tianaju asked me to bring you this. You must not open it until tonight." Simone then gave me a little green box tied with a ribbon, and then added, "I have to go now to prepare for the wedding. Good bye, Welusa. It was nice seeing you again."

She then flew out through the window and was gone.

The box was three inches long and about an inch wide. I put it away with my manuscript and lay there awake until my mother called me for breakfast. I spent the afternoon down town with my friends and came home about six. My mother had my suit of clothes all pressed and set out for me. I looked at them and said to myself, "Thank goodness it's a nice, fine night."

I had a wash, cleaned my teeth and trimmed my beard. I reluctantly put my suit of clothes on, put my little box into my jacket pocket and went downstairs to my parents. They both said I looked grand. My mother tried to give me a flower for my jacket, but I said, "No, it's okay. I don't want a flower." I kissed her goodbye, and set out off up the Keeper's Hill with my father shouting, "Have a nice time son."

I shouted back, "Thanks dad, I'll try too."

I hurried up the hill to the top, picked up my tent and erected it out of site. I lay there until dark then strolled over to a bench and sat down looking out at the valley below. I decided to wait until midnight to open my box so I took it out of my pocket and held it in my hand. It was nice and peaceful sitting there watching the flickering oil lamps and listening to the odd cry of a fox and the occasional hoot of a tawny owl. As I sat there I heard Cliff the Town Crier shout out the eleven o'clock news. There was no moon out but the stars were in their millions. In fact I have never seen so many.

I said to myself, "I wonder what's happening in Fairyland now? I bet she looks amazing. Well I told her that I would be with her in spirit, so I'll just close my eyes and think of us laughing and chatting during our time together."

I sat there, far away, talking and listening to her say, "Welusa what are you doing sitting there?"

I laughed and said, "Waiting for you to poke me in the back. I could do with a mattress right now and a blanket."

Then I remembered as she asked, "What would you do or say if I wasn't a fairy?"

I sighed and said, "That night I would have kissed you and told you that I loved you. Now I only wish I had."

I began to feel sad again after hearing her say, "When you asked me to marry you, why did you tell me you were only joking?"

I sighed again, shook my head and said, "I wasn't joking. I really did want to marry you."

I could even smell her lovely perfume now as I listened to her ask, "Do you want to know a secret? It was you I fell in love with and when you asked me to marry you, I did say I will. I wonder what I would say if you asked me again?"

The moment I heard her say this, my hand began to tingle. I opened my eyes and saw that my little box was sparkling. I quickly opened it and to my surprise inside was a little soft purple thistle. I got up and quickly turned around. My heart leapt with joy, for there hovering in the middle of a soft dome of light, on top of a sea of purple heather, was my beautiful smiling Tianaju the Emerald Queen of Children.

She was dressed in a shimmering white wedding gown, with a long wavering train. Her radiant smile once again was lighting up her beautiful face from underneath a small white glimmering veil, which was being held in place by a glistening purple tiara. Her long blond hair was hanging down in ringlets over her elegant lily white shoulders, and in her lovely hands she was holding a bouquet of soft purple thistles. As I moved closer I could see, lying gently around her delicate neck, was a twinkling purple thistle, looped on a silver chain.

She gently set down amongst the heather and beamed her beautiful smile.

I slowly walked up to her and went down on my knee, kissed the little thistle and offered it to her saying, "I love you Tianaju. Will you marry me?"

She gently took the thistle, placed it into her bouquet, smiled and said, "I am. I love you Welusa."

I stood up in amazement as she added, "All of Fairyland is waiting for us. We only have fifteen minutes left, so are you coming?"

I gently held her arms, gazed into her eyes, smiled and replied, "Well I might."

She smiled her beautiful smile again and said, "Bet your life you are."

Then, as she looked around at the heathers, all their lovely flowers floated up and covered the whole mountainside with a beautiful purple mist. When the mist slowly disappeared I saw to my absolute joy that there waiting for us, was Nabalion and Lianga. They were harnessed up, one behind the other, with Nabalion in front, to a sparkling green and purple coach, in the shape of a thistle. At that point my heart had never been so happy because I knew then that everything I longed for was really happening. The next thing I knew I was sitting alongside my beautiful Fairy Queen, holding her hand, heading for the new moon and Fairyland, looking forward to my first kiss.

Yours Truly,

Welusa Laycvcy

24th / February / 1889

Lightning Source UK Ltd.
Milton Keynes UK
UKOW06f0915041115

262058UK00001B/25/P